"Ryker, thanks for helping Honor tonight."

"She's going to love learning that way. And carving pumpkins as a reward was a great idea, too."

"Hopefully it will make it easier on both of you. You've already done so much for her. Maybe for next week's reward, you two can come out to the horse farm. Or I can take Honor for the day so we're not monopolizing your time."

"I don't mind going." Ryker had been talking about his work in such fond terms that Charlie wouldn't mind seeing the place—or spending time with Ryker in his element.

Still, she was beginning to fear that her *like* meter regarding him was slipping into the red zone. The last thing Charlie needed was a lopsided relationship with him. And she couldn't just ask Ryker if he felt anything for her because that would make their time together with Honor incredibly awkward.

So, Charlie would do what made the most logical sense. She'd bury anything blooming inside of her and focus on what mattered.

Which was Honor. Not herself…

Jill Lynn pens stories filled with humor, faith and happily-ever-afters. She's an ACFW Carol Award–winning author and has a bachelor's degree in communications from Bethel University. An avid fan of thrift stores, summer and coffee, she lives in Colorado with her husband and two children, who make her laugh on a daily basis. Connect with her at jill-lynn.com.

Books by Jill Lynn

Love Inspired

Colorado Grooms

The Rancher's Surprise Daughter
The Rancher's Unexpected Baby
The Bull Rider's Secret
Her Hidden Hope
Raising Honor

Falling for Texas
Her Texas Family
Her Texas Cowboy

Visit the Author Profile page at Harlequin.com.

Raising Honor

Jill Lynn

LOVE INSPIRED
INSPIRATIONAL ROMANCE

LOVE INSPIRED®
INSPIRATIONAL ROMANCE

PLEASE RECYCLE
THIS PRODUCT IS RECYCLABLE

Recycling programs
for this product may
not exist in your area.

ISBN-13: 978-1-335-48831-2

Raising Honor

Copyright © 2020 by Jill Buteyn

This edition published by arrangement with Harlequin Books S.A.

For questions and comments about the quality of this book,
please contact us at CustomerService@Harlequin.com.

Love Inspired
22 Adelaide St. West, 40th Floor
Toronto, Ontario M5H 4E3, Canada
www.Harlequin.com

Printed in U.S.A.

But Jesus said, Suffer little children,
and forbid them not, to come unto me:
for of such is the kingdom of heaven.
—*Matthew* 19:14

To the women who support me and love me and put up with me. Thank you for being my girls. I can't imagine life without you.

Chapter One

Charlie Brightwood had never looked into the eyes of a child and known their livelihood depended on her... until now.

Until now, she'd only visited the park in the small town of Westbend, Colorado, with her friend's little boy. Until now, she'd shoved down the ache inside her screaming for a child of her own. Until now, she'd planned to do the whole shebang in order—marriage and then the baby carriage.

But everything had changed when she'd felt the pull to foster a child. She had a loving heart and home. Why not fill that void with a kid who needed her as much as she needed them? Truly, God had laid the idea on her so heavily that she hadn't been able to budge it loose. She'd prayed and prayed and *prayed* for direction and had finally begun the process. She'd taken the leap to foster still not knowing if it was the right thing to do but trusting God to show her.

She'd read all of the things and asked all of the questions. She knew how hard it was going to be.

She knew she'd likely fall for a child and then have to give them back, shattering herself in the process.

She knew how scared she was.

She knew how easily she could mess it up.

The only thing she didn't know was what was running through Honor Sloan Delaney's head. The girl had been on lockdown since her arrival, only uttering eleven words in forty-five hours.

In the last year, Honor's mom had lost her job and replaced it with a meth addiction. The girl had come to Charlie's with only one outfit, no shoes and a stuffed bunny that had never seen the inside of a washing machine.

At three feet six inches tall and weighing thirty pounds soaking wet, a strong gust of wind could scoot the five-year-old a block. Her gorgeous, ocean-blue eyes haunted Charlie with the stories she'd yet to spill, and her shoulder-length dark chocolate hair fell in ringlets. It had been a mess of snarls when she'd arrived at Charlie's and had taken three rounds of conditioner to untangle.

Charlie wanted to wrap Honor in a protective hug and never let her go back into the big, bad world that would land a little one in a stranger's home, lost, confused, scared.

For the past few minutes, Honor had been cautiously swinging, the mountains rising clear and bright as her backdrop, the blue September sky filled with warm sunlight and littered with the occasional white cloud. Charlie hadn't known anyone could swing cautiously until observing the girl's careful movements and subdued enjoyment. But now her swing had come to a stop, as if she'd forgotten she was even on the thing. She stared off at nothing, misplaced, alone. Sealed in a realm Charlie had yet to break into.

After rising from the bench, Charlie rounded the swing. "Want a push?" She kept her voice gentle, hoping not to startle Honor. It worked, and she earned another nod. Nods were better than nothing, right? Or was her lack of response a sign that Charlie was a terrible foster parent already?

This was where a husband would come in handy. Charlie could ask his advice. They could pray together. She wouldn't have tossed and turned for hours by herself last night wondering if she'd made a mistake.

"Higher?" Her question earned another affirmative bobble, and Charlie gripped the chain and dragged it back before letting go and earning the faintest hint of delight from Honor.

Charlie often wondered if she'd missed out on her elusive partner, best friend, husband, because she'd been too busy building a business. If they were like ships that had passed on a dark ocean and now it was too late to find each other.

For her thirtieth birthday, instead of wishing for a man, Charlie had prayed for a child.

If God didn't have a partner for her, she would be okay. But she wasn't sure she'd survive not having children. Fostering was her first step into that world, though of course she had no idea how this situation with Honor would end up. How long she'd have the girl. If she'd ever be available for adoption or if her mom would figure out her life and gain back custody.

So many questions.

Charlie had a successful garage and was working on opening a place next door that would serve coffee and sweets and some light fare. A place to wait and even work while your car was being diagnosed and fixed. Another stream of income. Charlie was good at business, but she'd never been good at love. Well…she didn't even know if that was true, because she'd never had the chance to try.

But she had no doubts that she could love a child. Maybe too much.

An older Ram 1500 screeched into the parking lot adjacent to the playground, the driver slamming so hard on the brakes that the vehicle rocked in place for a few seconds. A man killed the truck engine and jumped out, boots landing on the pavement with a thud that raced across the ground and sent a shiver up Charlie's spine.

Despite it being a Wednesday afternoon, the park was empty but for them. She hadn't considered that dangerous until now.

Like something out of a nightmare, he beelined straight toward them. Charlie checked the pockets of her shorts. No Mace. Nothing to protect them if he was crazy. And based on the fact that there was no one else around and he was still coming at them…the thought wasn't ludicrous.

The chain slid through her grasp, and Charlie rounded Honor and took a wide stance a few feet in front of her.

"Can I help you?" she called out, but he showed no recognition of hearing her.

He was within ten yards now. Late twenties in age, she would guess. Dressed in a wrinkled T-shirt that sported an outline of the state of Texas, jeans and boots, he had messy, dark roast hair and cobalt eyes that were reminiscent of Honor's. Could this be her father?

No. The caseworker, Angela, had said the man hadn't been involved in the girl's life since birth.

Still, he continued their way like a freight train, brooding, laser focused—as if he could see through her to Honor. He didn't acknowledge Charlie at all.

"Hey!" He was about to plow right by her when she grabbed his arm, fingers grazing a tattoo that scrawled across his forearm. "What do you think you're doing?"

He paused, in shock, as if he hadn't noticed her before this second.

Angry eyes met hers and held. "Who are you and why do you have my niece with you? Honor?" He peered around her. "It's Uncle Ryker."

His niece? If an uncle existed, then why wasn't Honor with him? Charlie's trust level regarding anything this stranger said was currently at *not going to happen.*

"She's in my care. Who are you and why do you think barreling at us is any way to handle a situation like this?"

His chest puffed like a rooster about to peck. He wouldn't lay a hand on her, would he? Charlie wasn't versed in combat—she and her brother, Finn, had never fought physically over anything—but if it came down to it, she wouldn't let anyone get to Honor Sloan Delaney. Not on her watch.

Her right hand closed in a just-in-case fist. "You need to back off." Charlie hadn't gotten to be a female mechanic in a world full of boys by bowing to whatever hardship or roadblock had risen in her way. "I don't know who you are, despite what you say, and so, no, you're not going to get anywhere near Honor right now. You need to calm down." She kept her voice low and cool though her gut was bubbling with white-hot anger.

"I don't know who *you* are, and I don't care what you think. Get out of my way. I want to see my niece." His demand clipped out, and the fury radiating from him shot panic across Charlie's tense nerves.

"Is that a threat?" She scanned for backup—for anyone who could step in. If this man wanted Honor, he could snatch her up and run and Charlie would never be able to overpower him—no matter how much she desired to do exactly that. "If you have any actual claim to being a relative of Honor's, then spouting your mouth off right now isn't going to help anything. You need to call Angela Turner. She's in charge of Honor's case. If you have a beef with the decisions she's made thus far, then you need to contact her."

Honor had gotten down from the swing and now peeked around Charlie's legs, one sweet arm wrapped around her knees as if she was her protector.

I'm trying to be, Honor. I promise I'm doing my best.

"Uncle Ryker?" Honor's sweet, innocent and rarely used voice broke the tension.

Two words, all for this man? So, his claims were true…or somewhere close to true. Maybe he was a friend of Honor's mom that she called an uncle. Charlie didn't know the details. And nothing made his behavior just now acceptable.

She fisted her hands to stem their shaking, clenching her teeth to prevent chattering. Adrenaline had taken over her body.

The man—Ryker—dropped to his knees. "Hi, Honor. I'm sorry it took me so long to get here after your mama—" His voice cracked and quit working.

Honor took a step toward him, and he tugged her into a hug that the girl didn't fight.

He could take off with her. I have to stop this from continuing. The man might be an uncle of sorts, but if Honor wasn't already in his care, that meant Angela or the system or someone hadn't deemed him a safe place for the girl.

"Let her go. Please. I have no idea who you are—"

"You just heard it straight from her mouth." His icy-hot stare met hers over Honor's shoulder.

He stood but kept hold of Honor's hand.

"Do you need some help over there?" A man walking his dog paused on the sidewalk flanking the park.

"Yes," Charlie called out. "Can you keep an eye on him while I make a phone call? Make sure he doesn't leave with her. Thank you."

The dog walker nodded, letting his golden Labrador sniff the grass.

Ryker released a guttural growl. "I wouldn't do that."

"Let's hope that's true." Charlie had no idea what the man was capable of and if part of the reason Honor was in protective services was because he wasn't fit to be her caregiver. She dialed Angela. No answer. She sent a panicked text, detailing what was happening. Still no answer.

When Ryker took a step back while still grasping Honor's hand, visions of him disappearing with the girl roared to life.

Charlie began dialing the police, but her phone rang before she could hit Send.

"Angela. I'm so glad you called me back. There's a man here who says he's Honor's uncle."

"I am!" She rolled her eyes at his outburst.

"We're at the park, and I'm freaking out that he's going to take off with Honor."

"I said I wouldn't do that." Another eruption, and yet his grip on his supposed niece didn't loosen. Honor's chin wobbled, and her eyes turned glossy. How many messy problems did she have to handle in a matter of days?

"Okay." Why did Angela sound so calm? "Can you let me talk to him?"

"Yes. Hang on." Charlie handed over her phone, not sure she'd ever see it again. But she'd much rather sacrifice it than the girl.

The uncle launched into an explanation about how Honor's mother was his half sister. How he lived in Texas and had driven straight to Colorado to get Honor when he heard the news. How he was family and should be the one taking care of Honor. He even lobbed his anger toward Angela, telling her it was her fault for not locating him right away.

Based on the way he cringed after that, Charlie would guess Angela didn't take well to that accusation.

Next came a bunch of *ah-huh*s and *okay*s. The dog walker who'd come to her rescue continued on his way with a wave as Ryker quieted and calmed.

"Here." He shoved the phone back at her. "She says we're supposed to meet her at her office right now."

He knelt in front of Honor again. "You ride with—" He glanced up.

"Charlie," she filled in. Not that it was a proper introduction by any means.

"You ride with Charlie, and I'll meet you over there."

Honor nodded solemnly, and Charlie's chest broke open. Obviously, the man had some influence in her life. She seemed to know him. Perhaps Charlie's first fostering experience would be over as quickly as it had started. She'd read plenty about the system wanting kids to be with family if at all possible. But while this Ryker might have shared blood running through his veins, that didn't mean he was the right home for Honor.

Charlie was consistent and calm and safe…and this Ryker guy had just shown himself to be anything but.

His niece had better not suffer because of his stupid actions.

Ryker Hayes found a parking spot near the caseworker's office and inhaled deeply before dumping his tired, haggard body out of the cab of his truck.

Once he'd heard about Kaia being charged with neglect and Honor being taken from her, he'd driven all night from Texas, only stopping once to grab an hour of sleep. Why hadn't his sister called him when she'd first started having trouble? Why hadn't she let him know she needed help?

According to her neighbor, who *had* found a way to contact him after Honor had been removed from Kaia's care, his sister had gone off the deep end in the last few months. Sounded like she'd had a bad breakup and had plummeted downhill after. She'd started getting high on repeat, and Honor had suffered because of her stupid actions.

Ryker knew all too well about terrible relationships from watching his mother flip through them. And he knew all too well how they'd affected him as a kid.

Phone calls and texts with his sister had faded to nonexistent since spring, and he hadn't investigated why. He should have hopped in his truck months ago and driven up here to figure out what was going on. If he had, maybe Honor would be with him right now instead of a stranger.

Still, Ryker could admit he'd handled the situation at the park terribly. With the lack of sleep and his panic over the whereabouts and safety of his niece, to roll into town and see her at the park, right in front of him…he'd lost his mind. At first he'd thought he was hallucinating or imagining the little girl on the swing was Honor. But once he'd pulled into the lot, he'd known.

And now he had the sinking impression he was about to pay for blowing his temper.

Inside the quiet, air-conditioned office, he found a woman—must be the caseworker—sitting across from the redhead behind a massive oak desk.

"Where's Honor?"

"She's in the playroom, putting together a puzzle. I didn't want her in here for this discussion." The social worker wore blue glasses and a crisp white button-up shirt. Ryker suddenly felt very in need of a shower. He must look wrecked after driving all night. No wonder the redhead had reacted to him like he was a monster.

"Sit. Please." She motioned to the open chair.

Ryker obeyed. The woman next to him smelled like a strange mix of motor oil and lemons. He shook his head. That couldn't be right. What was her name again? Claire? Kate? No. That wasn't it. He might not be able to remember her name, but he'd never forget the fear that had burned into him from her evergreen eyes during their encounter at the park.

The fact that he'd frightened her ate at Ryker's core. He wasn't like the men his mom had brought home. He didn't lose it like them. Only he'd just gotten way too close to their behavior for his own comfort.

"Charlie told me a little about what happened at the park." Angela's head tilted to the right, eyes morphing to concerned slits. "I'd like to hear your version."

Charlie. That was her name. It fit. Ryker resisted glancing her way. He could only imagine the earful she'd given Angela at her arrival. The fact that she'd beaten him here by any amount of time did not bode well for him.

"I live in Texas, and when I heard what had happened with Honor, I drove straight here. I didn't know anything about her whereabouts or if she was okay. I drove all night without sleeping, so when I rolled into town, I can admit, I was a mess. And there I am, driving down Main and I see a little girl who looks like Honor. When I realized it *was* her… I didn't handle the situation well. I wasn't going to take her or do anything. I just…had to see her, to make sure she was okay."

The arms next to him stayed crossed, but Angela, at least, listened intently.

"Can I have Honor? Can I take care of her while Kaia is—" Ryker shook his head. "Getting her life back together." If that was even a possibility. He didn't know how far gone his sister was. Kaia was always getting into scrapes. Ryker could have easily headed down the same path, but he'd been rescued by a brown-eyed beauty. Kaia had not. When she'd reached high school, their mom had sent her to Colorado to live with her father. She'd ended up in Westbend because of a boyfriend—Honor's dad—and had stayed after he'd taken off.

His sweet little niece didn't deserve any of the mess she'd been born into. Ryker had met Honor a few times when he'd visited his sister, and they'd video called, too. She obviously knew him and remembered him if she'd come right to him at the park. That had to count for something, didn't it?

"I'm sure you can understand that your behavior just now has greatly damaged your chances in that regard." Angela's brow furrowed. "We do focus on reuniting children with their families, but you have quite a bit to prove."

"I will. I can. I promise, I'm not normally a hothead."

A snort sounded from next to him. Charlie sat up in her chair when he glanced her way, as if she hadn't realized she'd made the noise out loud.

Ryker continued. "I'll do whatever it takes to prove that I'm capable and dependable for Honor. And I'm sorry for my behavior at the park." The apology should be directed at Charlie, but Ryker didn't dare glance in her direction again. She might throw that punch she'd been fisting and considering earlier during their run-in.

Angela's sigh wasn't promising. "You said you live in Texas? What do you do there?"

"I work at a ranch. The Circle M in Fredericksburg."

Angela scribbled a note in what must be Honor's file. "You live by yourself?"

He cringed. "No… I live in a house with a few other guys." There'd been no reason to have his own place before now. Especially since the job was simply that. He wanted to do more. Work with horses, definitely. Maybe even teens. He'd ignored that tug over the years, telling himself to simply be grateful to have a consistent paycheck and a good employer, but it had never fully erased itself. Horses had made such an impact on him, it only made sense that he'd want to work with them on a regular basis, not just in the capacity he did as a ranch hand.

Angela shifted her glasses to peer over the top. "That doesn't sound like an ideal situation. Honor needs to have her own bedroom and space. And no other adult roommates who aren't approved."

"Should I go check on Honor?" Charlie asked. "You probably don't need me here for this discussion."

The woman thought her keeping Honor was in the bag…and she was probably right.

Angela held up a finger. "Hang on, Charlie. I think I'm going to need you."

Great. What did that mean? Ryker's chance to care for Honor was slipping through his fingers faster than a tornado over flat land.

"I can move to Colorado. I'll find a job and a place with a bedroom for her. She's my niece. I'll do anything for her."

Angela made more notes on her paperwork. He waited, that whole pins-and-needles description tormenting him. Ryker couldn't let his niece go to someone else. This Charlie might be great…or she might be horrible. He didn't know anything about her. And she wasn't his concern. Honor was.

"Based on your behavior earlier, and now the fact that you can't provide what Honor needs in terms of a place to live, I can't allow your request to care for her."

His chest opened in a gaping wound. He'd appeal. He'd get a lawyer. Find another way. Ryker wasn't going to just give up on Honor. She needed someone consistent. She needed family. He was both of those things.

"But," Angela continued, and both he and Charlie leaned forward in their chairs. "I am going to grant you visitation rights with her while you figure out how to prove that, one, you're not the guy who just stomped across a playground and had strangers stopping to see if Charlie or Honor needed protection, two, you can provide the type of home she needs, and three, you can complete the paperwork and courses required."

The panic stitched back up, slowly, carefully. Hope tasted extra sweet right about now. "Thank you. I promise that I'll prove I can take care of her. That I'm the right home for her."

Ryker was probably offending the woman next to him on repeat. But then again, if she'd agreed to foster Honor—who wasn't up for adoption—wouldn't she have known the situation wasn't permanent?

"This is where you come in, Charlie." Angela turned to her. "Usually we'd have a visitation supervisor for a situation like this—and often a house where the visitations could happen—but we're short staffed and spread through three towns in this county. We're not set up for anything like that in Westbend. If we wait, it will take longer to make a visit happen, and I do think *if* Mr. Hayes has an established relationship with Honor like he claims, then any time spent with him would be beneficial for her. I'm wondering if you'd be willing to supervise the visits. You all can come here and use our playroom. You can go to the park or get ice cream. He can come to your apartment. Whatever you feel comfortable with."

Charlie's forest green eyes widened with each bit of information from Angela. "I don't know that I feel comfortable with any of that. I don't know him." She swallowed, not glancing in his direction. "And my first encounter wasn't pleasant."

Ryker beat back a groan. He'd probably resembled a gorilla tearing over to Honor like he had. He hadn't even noticed Charlie until she'd stepped in front of him and interrupted his path.

"It's okay if you make that choice. Mr. Hayes can wait. He's the one who chose to act as he did."

Ryker's world crumbled. He'd been an idiot. He wasn't that man. He'd just…lost it. Lost his mind, really. He was good for Honor, he knew that. And at least she'd be with family if she were with him. He was a good uncle. He just needed the chance to show them that. But if Charlie didn't give him the opportunity— and why should she?—he'd be stuck.

"Please." His voice cracked on the request. He twisted to face Charlie. "I understand how awful the situation at the park was, but I promise I'm not that person. If you had a niece and you didn't know where she was or if she was okay and then saw her out of the blue like I did…doesn't that make any sense? I'm not making excuses. I'll atone for my behavior. Just…please give me a chance to do that."

It took her one thousand years to answer. Her exhale was long, her head shaking, her lids shuttered. "Fine." It came out bitter, but it was the best word he'd ever encountered.

He could work with fine. And he'd find a way to prove who he really was and that he could provide the kind of home Honor needed.

His niece deserved that. Actually, she deserved a loving mom and dad who made good choices and didn't neglect her needs—emotional or physical. But since that option wasn't on the table, Ryker would do his absolute best to provide for her.

Right after he was given permission to do exactly that.

Chapter Two

Charlie had really, really, *really* wanted to say no to Angela's request. She had absolutely no desire to spend even an iota of her time with Ryker Hayes. Did she believe he was the good guy he touted himself to be? No. Did she think he'd even show tonight for his first visitation? Doubtful.

But she'd agreed, because at least then she would have done her part. She would have made the effort—for Honor's sake.

Charlie checked the clock. Ten minutes until she had to leave to grab Honor from school. The girl could ride the bus, but Charlie had been picking her up this week because she was concerned about how Honor was handling everything. Plus, with Honor's uncle in town, Charlie's intuition was flashing like a massive red alarm that refused to quit.

Ryker had explained himself and apologized during the meeting with Angela. He'd been contrite, and Charlie no longer feared he'd snatch Honor and run.

But she still trusted him as much as she did a DPS6 transmission.

"Scott—you good if I take off in a minute?"

Yes, Scott technically worked for her, but he was fresh out of school and new to her shop. He was only twenty, but she'd liked what she saw in him. He'd tinkered with tractors and mowers and equipment on his parents' farm growing up. And since Charlie would soon be getting stretched in so many directions with her plan to remodel and open a café next door to the shop, she needed another body working on cars.

Scott poked his head out from under the back of the car where he was replacing a fuel pump. "I'm good. Tell Honor to pop in and say hi to me when she comes home."

It had been four days since Honor had come to live with Charlie, and already Scott had a knack for coaxing a smile out of the little girl. Charlie could do the same on occasion, too, but not as consistently as she liked.

After removing her gloves and washing up, Charlie rubbed lemon cream lotion into her hands and then checked on the progress next door. Before she'd purchased the spot, it had been a run-down building, empty for who knew how long. She'd finally found a contractor whose prices were fair market and who came highly recommended. His crew was beginning to demo this week, and based on the mess, they'd been hard at work today. She planned to keep a lot of the bones—the brick walls, the worn wood floors. She wanted a simple design with clean lines and not a lot of fuss.

When Charlie had found out the space was for sale, her temptation had been two parts. One, she liked business. Had a head for business. And two, it would keep more of her customers' money siphoning into her pocket and not running out the shop door. So many people wanted a place to work while their car was getting fixed. The café—which she had yet to name—would provide that. She wasn't going to compete with the food at The Fork and Spoon or restaurants like that. This would be more of a work space—one that served a handful of snack and sandwich items beyond drinks. At least… that was her current plan. It might morph as construction progressed.

At the back of the building, she jogged up the steps to the two-bedroom apartment she now shared with Honor that resided above Charlie's Garage. The place wasn't large by any means, but she didn't need much beyond a small living room and kitchen in addition to the bedrooms. She and Honor were good sharing one bathroom. Charlie's brother, Finn, was her most consistent guest, but he'd be fine securing other arrangements when he was in town. Their parents lived in Durango and had visited her in July, so she likely wouldn't see them until the holidays.

Finn had been introduced to the town of Westbend when he'd worked a stint at a local guest ranch run by the Wilder family. He'd decided it was a good place to settle and then had taken a job on an oil rig in order to save enough money to afford his own spread. After Charlie sold her previous garage in Colorado Springs, she'd decided to settle near her brother when opening a new shop last spring. Finn had been searching for a ranch near Westbend for ages and would hopefully find the right one soon. She was ready for him to live close to her, since he was a majority of the reason she'd opened her garage in this town.

The September weather had yet to cool down and was consistently running in the eighties, so Charlie wore shorts and a striped V-neck T-shirt to pick up Honor. Warmth heated her shoulders as she drove her 1967 Mustang convertible to the elementary school, which was located on the far side of town. When she arrived, Charlie drove through the pickup line. Honor spotted the car and broke into a grin—the whole reason Charlie had driven it. Turned out the girl enjoyed the convertible as much as Charlie did.

Honor went around to the passenger side and climbed into the back seat.

"Hey, Honor. How was your day?"

She buckled into her booster seat as Charlie moved slowly ahead. "Good."

One word.

"Did anything great happen today?"

Her head shook. No words.

"Did anything terrible happen today?"

Her head swung side to side again, and then she glued her gaze on the mountains as they eased out of the lot, her posture relaxing as if the end of school was the best part of her day.

Honor didn't talk on the drive home, and Charlie tried desperately not to care. Would she ever get through to the girl? Or would she be gone before they were able to forge any meaningful connection? Not for the first time, Charlie wondered if she'd done the right thing in choosing to foster parent. There were other ways to bring a child into her life. She could have looked into adoption. Or refused to foster unless the child's parental rights had already been terminated.

But when Angela had called about Honor, Charlie had known that she was supposed to say yes. Her gut had given her The Signal. Even if her heart crumbled in the process, this was where she was supposed to be.

She parked in her personal garage, located across the alley behind the shop, and waited for Honor to grab her backpack and climb out. For full-day kindergarten, there wasn't much for homework besides reading, so it didn't usually contain more than a lunch, but Honor adored the backpack. Charlie wasn't sure what she'd used before coming to live with her. They'd bought the backpack together during their first outing. There'd been plenty with characters on them, bright and a bit atrocious in Charlie's opinion, but Honor had chosen one with stars on it. Simple and pretty.

"Your uncle Ryker is coming by tonight to see you." Charlie managed to make the announcement without choking on the vile taste it left in her mouth. She still wasn't okay with any of this, but she refused to be labeled a quitter. When Charlie had said yes to fostering, she'd said yes to a whole world she knew very little about. And she'd figure out a way to roll with the changes. Somehow.

Honor simply nodded.

Charlie hadn't heard a peep from the girl's uncle since their encounter on Wednesday night, and she was both relieved and shocked by that. Maybe he wasn't the jerk he'd been on the playground. Then again, maybe he was simply trying to act a certain way in order to gain the right to care for his niece.

Angela had investigated Ryker's story before giving Charlie the all clear for the visitation today. Ryker and Kaia were half siblings. Same mom, different dads.

At twenty-eight, Ryker was a handful of years older than Kaia. He didn't appear to be struggling with the same issues as his half sister, but Charlie knew very little about him besides what Angela had shared.

She both wanted and didn't want the man to show up tonight. No for her. And *maybe* yes for Honor. Maybe. If Ryker was a good man. If he was who he claimed to be. If his presence in Honor's life was helpful and not a hindrance. But the jury on all of that was still out.

Charlie had just finished putting away dinner—chicken and vegetables, of which Honor ate precisely six bites—when a knock sounded on her door. She checked through the peephole. The man had cleaned up since their last run-in. Ryker wore a short-sleeved plaid shirt with jeans and boots. He'd shaved and lost the haggard appearance that had been clinging to him when he'd rolled into town. A long, jagged sigh ripped from Charlie's lungs. Didn't matter if he was as shiny as a brand-new penny. Underneath he was still the same guy. Why had she agreed to this again?

Charlie had considered telling Ryker to meet them at the park in order to avoid having him show up at her home address, but since she lived over Charlie's Garage, there was no hiding for her or Honor. She wasn't sure how to feel about that—about any of this.

"Honor, your uncle is here." Her call was answered by thundering footsteps that surprised Charlie with their velocity.

When she opened the front door, Honor flew into Ryker's arms. He scooped her up, her little bare feet dangling. "How's my girl?"

Honor didn't answer, which perversely gave Charlie a lift. If she'd started chattering like crazy, it would have crushed her. Even though she did wish for that kind of happiness for Honor.

Ryker put Honor down, acknowledging Charlie for the first time. "Charlotte." His tone held a sliver of spite.

"Only my mom calls me that." When she'd been little, her granddad had begun calling her Charlie, and much to her mom's chagrin, the moniker had stuck. Charlie preferred the shorter version. It fit her better.

"Sorry." *Please.* He was miles away from that apology. "It was on the paperwork that Angela sent over to me." Ryker was still standing on the landing, as she'd yet to invite him in. If Charlie gave the door a hefty shove, it would likely stop just short of crushing his nose. Interesting. She didn't usually experience such a tug toward violence. His eyebrows arched as if he could read her thoughts, and she scrambled her telltale features that so often gave her away.

"I thought maybe we could walk to the park tonight." Charlie didn't feel comfortable having Ryker in her place as of yet. Angela had offered the playroom at her office, but that wouldn't excite Honor. This did, according to her nodding head and bouncing legs.

Charlie understood the predicament that Angela was in and the huge caseload she was under. And that they weren't staffed for covering visits in a small town like Westbend. She understood it, but that didn't mean she had to like it. The playground was a good compromise. They could walk there from her apartment, which avoided the awkwardness of riding somewhere in a car together. Plus, the park made Honor happy…or at least not unhappy.

Charlie didn't love that they'd be heading back to the scene of the crime—where Ryker had barreled at them—but there weren't many other options. She and

Honor had gotten ice cream last night, so it didn't seem prudent to do the same a second evening in a row.

"In this?" Ryker turned and scanned the sky. A couple dark clouds hovered over the mountains, but the rest was clear. The moisture would likely scoot by them to the north.

Honor tugged on Charlie's hand, her nod determined.

"Honor says yes. I say we do it."

What Charlie said, went. That's the lesson Ryker had learned so far. He'd mentioned numerous times on their walk to the park that his weather app had predicted rain, but he'd been ignored.

Kind of like right now.

Charlie was sitting on a bench, her nose in a book.

"Are you just going to read all night?"

The woman glanced up, a whole mess of emotions ranging from annoyance to exasperation scrunching her peaches-and-cream features. She wore an olive-and-white-striped T-shirt with shorts and espresso leather sandals. She was the definition of casual, but with her short red hair and those smoky evergreen eyes, she was incredibly unique.

Pretty.

No. Nope. *Do not go there, Ryker Hayes.* The absolute worst thing he could do right now was find the woman fostering Honor attractive.

His current and pressing mission was to gain the right to raise Honor in Kaia's absence. Nothing else mattered but finding a way to take care of her. He'd seen enough of his mom putting boyfriends first—before him and Kaia—to confirm he'd never travel that road. Romantic relationships complicated things, and Ryker refused to repeat his mother's broken patterns.

"This is your time with Honor," Charlie answered. "Just pretend I'm not here." *Easier said than done.* She gave a cool smile, then slipped behind her book shield once again. "I'm here for Honor. Not you." Her snarky whisper was quiet enough that she probably thought Ryker wouldn't catch it.

She'd be wrong.

He was torn between finding Charlie Brightwood amusing, distracting or problematic. That last one wouldn't be on the list if she wasn't a roadblock for him getting to care for Honor. But since Angela was nowhere near ready to put Honor in his care, Ryker should really be thankful for Charlie. His niece could have ended up in a much worse situation, but she'd been sent to live with the trusted town mechanic. Yes, Ryker had asked around about Charlie. No one had a bad thing to say about her.

He *was* glad for Honor's sake that she'd been placed with Charlie. But the woman's stellar reputation might make the battle for the right to care for Honor even tougher.

Family is the first choice, he reminded himself. Ryker had done some research, some digging. The system was supposed to try to place children with family members. He just had to get everything ready so that he was prepared for Honor. He needed an apartment. A job. Small, overwhelming things like that. In the last two days, he'd filled out a mountain of paperwork for Angela and had also contacted his boss back in Texas to notify him that he planned to stay in Colorado. Thankfully he'd been understanding. The Circle M had been a great

place to work, and Ryker hated leaving without notice.
If it weren't for Honor and this emergency situation, he
would never even consider it. Ryker had also asked his
roommates to box up his things and try to rent out his
room, since his lease wasn't up for another six months.

For all intents and purposes, he considered his move
to Colorado permanent. Even if Kaia did find a way to
correct her mistakes and gain back custody of Honor,
Ryker couldn't see himself leaving the state. He had to
live close to Honor from now on to make sure she was
okay. Somebody had to be a consistent adult for the girl.

His sweet niece flew down the slide, and when she
reached the bottom, Ryker whirled her in circles until
his arms needed a break. Honor's enjoyment was faint
but present, which Ryker considered a victory. She'd
been so quiet the other day and again tonight. It was as
if she'd lost her voice when she'd lost her mom. When
Ryker had talked to Honor over video call, she'd always
had a shyness, but she'd still been willing to communi-
cate and tell him something about her day. She was obviously struggling with being yanked from her mom, no
matter how lacking the situation had been. Rightfully
so. Kaia might make bad decisions from time to time,
but she loved Honor. Ryker still believed that to be true.

Without the Armijos, Ryker would have bumbled
along like his sister. Maybe even worse. The older couple had kept him occupied in junior high and high school
by having him help out with their horses. That had been
the first time Ryker had belonged. Anger over his mom's
choices and long string of equally bad boyfriends had
finally begun to drain out of him.

If not for the Armijos and their horses, Ryker had no
idea who he'd be right now. They were the ones who'd

introduced him to Jesus. They were the ones who'd encouraged him and fed him dinner. His mom had been present but usually distracted by whatever man was current in her life. She'd married Ryker's father and Kaia's father, but other than that, she'd gone through boyfriends like a kid did Goldfish crackers.

Once the Armijos sold the ranch, Ryker had switched to being a ranch hand at the Circle M, but his hidden desire had always been to work directly with horses again—to return his focus to the beautiful, calming creatures who had the capacity to turn a kid's murky heart pink and healthy.

But with Honor in his life, Ryker would be shelving that dream. Again. She was more important than anything or anyone else, and he'd take any job to be close to her, to be able to provide for her.

"Let's race, Uncle Ry." *Ry.* Kaia had always called him that. Honor must have picked up on it. His chest burned with resolve. *I'll figure out a way to take care of you, Honor. I promise.*

"Okay. Last one to the grass is a polka-dot unicorn."

Honor tore across the mulch while squealing, feet flying, curls doing the same, and Ryker jogged after her.

She reached the parched grass and turned, hands on her hips, claiming her win without saying a thing.

Sassy girl. "You're way too fast for me. I'm going to have to practice before we have a rematch."

Her sapphire eyes danced.

From the vicinity of the bench, a faint smile bent the portion of Charlie's lips that peeked out from under her book.

So, she was paying attention.

Ryker's skin heated. Despite the book shield, Charlie

was surely watching him like a hawk, documenting his every word and move, then packing them up and sending them on the express train to Angela.

This was his punishment for losing his mind. But even if he hadn't, it wasn't like Angela would have signed Honor's care over to him. She'd given him a list of things he had to change in order to make that happen. Angela certainly wasn't going to let Honor crash with him at the Lazy Bones Motel he was currently calling home. Ryker wouldn't, either. The place was a two on the cleanliness scale, and the decor left much to be desired. Since he was in a pinch and needed something cheap, it would do.

"Let's swing." Honor skipped away.

She could say *let's pick up trash* and he'd be in.

Ryker shoved his body between the chains and onto the plastic seat, pumping his legs along with Honor. Once she got going, she leaned back, her dark brown curls dancing in the breeze the swing created.

Carefree. Finally. If only the feeling would stay with her and sink into her bones. After a few minutes, she switched back to the slide and Ryker followed.

Boom! The sky crackled and heaved with thunder. From the top of the slide, Honor's eyes expanded to golf ball size. From the top of the *metal* slide…

"You'd better come down in case there's lightning. Come on."

She listened, zooming into his arms. He caught her, swinging her in a circle that earned rave reviews before depositing her on the ground. A fat drop landed on his head, and Ryker glanced to the sky. Those few dark clouds had produced babies. And then some. It was leaning toward dusk, too, so the light was disappearing by the second.

"We should probably head back." Charlie's call was interrupted by a flash and another even louder crash.

Honor latched on to his leg, and Ryker scooped her up. "It's okay, Hon. They're just bowling in heaven, remember?" That's what his mom had always told him when he'd been little and the noise had scared him.

The skies opened up and gushed down.

"Over here! There's an awning."

Ryker followed Charlie's yell and path. It landed them under the awning of the building next door. Rain slipped under as it came down sideways, but it was better than being exposed in the park.

Charlie peeked out from their protective cover. "Should we make a run for my place? Or wait it out?"

Another bout of lightning illuminated the night.

"I don't know how long this is supposed to last, but it's pretty rough right now. I think we'll have to wait it out for a bit." Ryker fought back the *I told you so* itching to jump from his tongue.

Honor whimpered in his arms, and he tucked her head against his shoulder. "It's okay, honey. You're fine. We're okay." It wasn't the best of situations, but they should be safe enough under the small cover. The lightning would focus on something taller, something metal. At least that's what he asked for in his silent prayer.

Pop-pop-pop. Small icy pebbles spit from the sky, drumming against the awning like horse hooves.

"I'm scared." Honor's wail ended on a cry, and Charlie ran a hand across her hair. It was soft and springy today—Charlie's doing, Ryker assumed. It had never looked this healthy when he'd video chatted with his sister. Ryker hated to think of Kaia losing custody of Honor as a good thing, but he also hated to think that Honor hadn't been getting the care she needed. Somewhere along the way, he'd failed them.

When he'd dropped by his sister's apartment after running into Honor and Charlie the other night, the landlord told him Kaia hadn't been paying her rent and had been in the process of being evicted. Most of her things were gone from the apartment, and the landlord had given him a couple of boxes of stuff that had been left. None of which looked to be of any value.

Ryker had questioned the neighbors as to Kaia's whereabouts, but no one had given him any clues as to where she'd gone. She'd been charged with neglect but not arrested, so she was probably afraid, not knowing what that meant. She'd run somewhere. Where was his sister now? And what was she doing?

Honor leaned in Charlie's direction, then crashed into the woman's arms. "It's okay, Honor." Charlie's hand raked gently over his niece's head time and time again. "It's just water and ice. It's not going to hurt us under here. It's just being loud and noisy. We should tell it to be quiet."

Slightly hopeful eyes peeked out from Charlie's shoulder.

"What do you think? Should we yell at the storm?"

Honor nodded, chewing on her thumbnail.

"Are you going to yell or just me?"

Honor pointed to Charlie…and then him. Ryker softened. "You think we should tell it to stop storming, huh?"

Her tiny teeth pressed into her top lip as her head bobbed again.

Charlie held his gaze directly, apologetically. "Sorry." Her mouth curved.

He laughed. "I'm in. Let's do this." They faced the wall of moisture, which had switched back to rain.

"Stop it, you big, bad, meany storm." Charlie went first, and Ryker's lips twitched.

He joined in. "Stop storming right now!"

A giggle followed. Honor had perked up. The rain sputtered, the roar notching down.

"Again!" Honor proclaimed. She waved her hand like a queen surveying her domain. Amusement threaded between Ryker and Charlie. It was the first time their communication wasn't bogged down with distrust.

They both yelled at the sky, pausing to laugh between exclamations. Strangely enough, Ryker found the whole thing enjoyable. Almost…therapeutic. Stress relief from the last few crazy days. When Charlie shouted that the storm was a "stinky, bratty, bossy-pants," Honor giggled and asked to be put down.

She stepped to the edge of the awning but not fully into the storm. Ryker would guess they were both intrigued by what she would do next.

Honor's pointer finger shook at the weather. "You stop it right now, sky! No more rain! Or lightning or thunder!" She barked the whole phrase out in a string, determination crowding her tiny, adorable features.

"Whoa. That was thirteen at once."

"Thirteen what?"

Honor began dipping the toes peeking out of her sandals into a puddle that had formed. She'd scooted far enough away that Charlie could answer quietly without her overhearing.

"Words. She hasn't been talking a lot."

Ah. "It's not you. I'm sure she's just struggling with being—"

"Ripped from her home and mother?"

"Yeah, exactly. Kaia means well, but she didn't have much of a chance growing up. Our mom wasn't the best at relationships, and she followed suit." Kaia's constant string of boyfriends had begun in junior high. Their mom's had started after the marriages to each of their fathers had failed. Ryker's world had become a revolving door of men. One in particular had messed with him, doing the most damage. The attacks when his mom hadn't been paying attention had been mainly verbal. Rarely physical. It was painful to revisit those memories, even now.

The Armijos and their horses had rescued him. But when Kaia had acted out in high school, Mom had sent her to Colorado to live with her dad, so she hadn't been able to follow Ryker's path. She'd never ended the downward cycle.

Once his sister reappeared, Ryker would know more about the next steps with Honor and whether she'd need care for months or years. And outside of that, nothing else mattered. Even the woman who'd taken Honor in and obviously already cared for her.

Sure, he felt a tug of attraction toward Charlie. Especially seeing her yell at the sky just now to make Honor smile, to lessen her fear. But he could easily bury that unwelcome spark of interest.

Honor was his main concern and focus. And Charlie, despite any intrigue she created in him, was not. If push came to shove and Ryker had to combat Charlie for the right to raise his niece in the absence of her mother, then that's exactly what he would do.

Chapter Three

Finding an apartment in Westbend that wouldn't break the bank along with the expenses moving would incur wasn't as easy as Ryker had hoped. He'd spent the weekend looking for an apartment and a job, and so far, nothing on either account.

There was also no news from Texas—no one interested in taking over his room and rent.

At this rate he'd end up moving back to Texas and having to fight for the right to raise Honor from there. He could only imagine how taxing that would be.

The apartment Ryker had just viewed was eerily close to Charlie's place. Only two blocks away. But then, Westbend wasn't *that* big. Everything would be too close for comfort—at least from Charlie's point of view.

His next visitation with Honor was tomorrow night. After the storm fiasco on Friday evening that had somehow turned out okay, he hadn't heard anything from Charlie. It wasn't her duty to keep him updated on Honor, he knew that, but at the same time, a little info would be nice.

"Let me know what you think of the place." The landlord—a quirky woman named Alma Dinnerson—had shown him the small two-bedroom, two-bath that took up one side of a duplex. It wasn't fancy, but it checked off the requirements on Angela's list, so it would do.

"I think the place is great." He carefully tiptoed into the portion of the conversation where everyone else had told him no. "I'm a good renter, easygoing, and I always pay on time. I have the first month's rent, but I don't have the security deposit yet. I'm moving here unexpectedly from Texas, and I'm waiting to get my deposit back from my place there so that I can use it here." Ryker did have some money in savings, but he couldn't drain all of that. Not when he didn't have a job in Westbend yet. "And I'm actually still looking for work here, too." Might as well lay all of his issues out for Alma, though between the two admissions, his chances of renting her place had likely just dropped to zero percent.

Alma studied him. "Got yourself in a bit of a predicament, do you?"

That was more than any of the other landlords had asked him.

"My sister—Kaia Delaney—lost custody of my niece, and I'm trying to find a place with a bedroom for her that will allow the state to let me keep her. I think she should be with family." Ryker wasn't above going for the sympathy vote. Especially if it benefited Honor. Which it would. Family was always best, right?

"I've met Kaia. She did some cleaning for a few of my other properties." How many places did this woman own? She was dressed in polyester pants and a flowered shirt with the kind of shoes that shouted 1960s nurse and arch support. And yet, she probably held more investments than the average banker. "Her daughter was a sweetheart. Quiet, but a good girl."

"Honor is amazing. She's struggling, of course, with everything going on, but I want to be as consistent for her as possible. If the caseworker lets me."

Alma nodded. "You're doing a good thing, Ryker Hayes." He sure hoped he was. He'd like to shake his sister, figure out what was going on with her, but she'd fallen off the face of the earth since his arrival in town.

"I tell you what. Let me think about it. I have another showing for this place tonight, and if that doesn't work, I'll consider you, even with all of your issues."

Ryker's grin inched into existence at the olive branch and offense rolled into one. It was true—he had boat-loads of issues right now.

"Okay, thanks. Let me know." They parted ways.

As Ryker jumped into his truck, his phone dinged with a text…from Charlie. He clicked on it.

Honor wants to go for a convertible ride. It's one of the only things she really seems to enjoy, and it's a nice evening.

Had she meant to send the text to someone else? Another ding followed.

She scrounged up enough words to tell me that she also wants you to go with us, and since I'm not an ogre, I can't refuse her.

His cheeks creased. No matter how much Charlie probably wanted to.

He should really continue his job hunt, but who would

be open or answering the phone on a Sunday night? He'd give it a rest for the evening, spend some time with his niece. After all, she was the reason he was here. He just hoped that he could find a way to stay, for both of their sakes.

I'm two blocks away looking at an apartment. I'll be right over.

When he arrived, Charlie and Honor were playing in the sandbox located near the back of the garage. She had a patio table with an umbrella set up, a grill under the stairs, a small patch of grass. Not a full-fledged back-yard, but what did that matter? Honor had likely gotten more attention with Charlie in the last handful of days than she had with Kaia in a month. Ryker stifled the internal sigh that whipped blame in his direction. He'd certainly dropped the ball on keeping up with his sister the last few months and checking on Honor.

Never again.

Charlie acknowledged him, and Honor waved. "Hi, Uncle Ry." She contentedly dug and moved sand.

"Hi, Hon." The temptation to join her was strong. Ryker hadn't played in a sandbox in a long, long while.

"Should we go for a ride?" Charlie asked, and Honor popped up, brushing her palms against her striped shorts.

Charlie led the way to what must be a personal garage in the back alley. She opened the roll-up door. "I'll back out since there's not a lot of space inside."

On the opposite side of the garage was a yellow FJ Cruiser. But what Charlie backed out was a collector Ford Mustang, candy-apple red and perfectly restored.

Ryker whistled. "Wow. Did you restore it yourself?" He was afraid to stick the worn boots and jeans residing on his body inside the pristine vehicle. Honor didn't have any of the same concerns. She climbed into the back seat like the car was her own personal play place, and Charlie didn't make a peep about her likely still sandy limbs or shoes. Impressive.

"With my granddad. When I was in high school. I didn't know it was my graduation gift until after we were done." Charlie handed Honor a hat and sunglasses, and she donned the items, looking adorable.

When he told her so, she beamed.

"Are you sure?" Ryker asked Charlie before getting in, dropping his voice.

He could understand why Charlie wouldn't want him around. They were basically enemies at this point. He'd been terrible to her at the park, and now he was fighting to take Honor from her. Charlie was obviously qualified as a caregiver for his niece, or she would never have been approved in the first place.

"Just get in."

Amusement surfaced as Ryker obeyed. "Yes, ma'am."

They found a radio station that Honor approved of and tooled out of town and into the hills surrounding Westbend. Ranches and cattle marked the land that ranged from green to brown and every shade in between. Definitely dryer than Texas, but it had an appeal all its own.

A small creek snaked through tall grasses, and Charlie parked to the side of the road. Ryker let Honor out of the back seat, and she ran over to a spot where a sandy bank kissed the water. She dipped her fingers in, screeching with pleasure over how cold it was.

"Done this with her before?"

Charlie had stayed behind the wheel, and she watched Honor for a few beats before answering. "Yep. She showed interest in the car and we ended up going for a ride. She's asked to do it again a couple of times. It's hard to know if she's okay. I mean, I know she's not okay, but I can't fix it, and that's the worst. For some reason a ride in the convertible is her happy place, so that's what we do."

Ryker's rib cage constricted. Charlie continued to surprise him. There'd been a moment that he'd considered her a villain just because of her proximity to Honor. Because she was caring for his niece instead of him. But she obviously wasn't in it for the money—he'd looked up what a foster parent made, and it wasn't even enough to cover costs, in his opinion. Charlie's heart must be the size of ten city blocks. And she was doing all of this on her own. Single. He'd been nosy and asked Angela, because he'd wanted to know if there were any other adults in Honor's life. Any other men, specifically. After what he'd been through with his mom's boyfriends, he'd had to know.

Honor ran in their direction. "I wanna see horses!" Ryker opened the door, and she climbed back into the car like a diva waiting for her entourage to catch up.

It was good to see her like this. Good to recognize the little girl who'd always demanded time with him across the screen on Kaia's phone. Showing him a dance move she'd learned or a terrible cartwheel that he'd obviously applauded. She was still in there. They just had to find a way to pull her out.

Exactly what Charlie had been doing.

Ryker buckled up again, and the car eased back onto

the road. "We found a horse farm the other day when we were out driving. It was Honor's favorite part."

His pulse jumped to attention. That hadn't come up in his job search. Which probably meant they weren't hiring. And even if they were...frustration sent his thudding heart crashing to the toes of his boots. He wasn't qualified to work at a horse ranch, since he didn't have experience training or selling or marketing horses.

You're never going to amount to anything. You're just a piece of trash your mama never wanted.

The memory from one of many encounters with his least favorite of his mom's boyfriends, Bruce, popped into his mind without permission. Over the years, Ryker had tried to combat the lies the man had spun, but despite his house-cleaning attempts, the web stayed, and he was the helpless fly glued to it.

They picked up speed, and Honor screeched and tugged on her hat. It must have loosened at the stop.

"Put the tie under your chin." Charlie motioned and yelled to her over the wind, and Honor secured it.

Before they'd left town, Charlie had wrapped a scarf around her short red hair and plunked on oversize sunglasses. "You look very Hollywood right now." Ryker hadn't meant to let his thoughts tumble out of his mouth. He also hadn't meant to find Charlie attractive. Failed on both accounts.

Her eyebrows joined forces. "Ha, right." He hadn't been joking, but her taking it that way might be a good thing.

She turned onto a dirt road that twisted and climbed.

Charlie slowed as they neared a spread that was flanked by white fences and littered with deep russet outbuildings. She stopped near the entrance and turned off the car. Ryker scooted his seat forward, and Honor scrambled out and began walking the fence line, talking to the horses. If only they could catch what she was saying.

"It's so great to hear her jabber, even if it's not to me."

"I was thinking the same." Ryker moved his seat back and stretched out his legs. "My sister isn't a bad person." He'd just blurted that out, hadn't he? But it was hard not to be on the defensive when it came to Kaia. Honor's first years had been good. Maybe not perfect, but Kaia had done okay, working for a cleaning business. Ryker wished his sister was around to explain to him how and when things had gone so sour. He'd called her father and left messages but had yet to hear back from him if he knew anything regarding Kaia's whereabouts. If she was okay.

The pained expression Charlie shot him was equal parts *really?* and *I don't want to hear it.*

Did she know that her face broadcasted her feelings to the next county?

"My childhood wasn't the easiest," Ryker continued. "And hers wasn't, either. Some people—" *and horses* "—rescued me, but no one ever did that for her. I tried, but…" He shrugged. Kaia had never met a bad decision she didn't like, and once she'd moved to Colorado, he'd lost the chance to influence her.

Charlie ran her hand absentmindedly over the steering wheel, her features softening with a hint of compassion. "I'm not judging. I'm just…" When she spoke, her voice was burdened. "She came to me with almost nothing, Ryker. She's five years old. She's practically a baby still."

A rock wedged in his throat, his swallow doing nothing to dislodge it. "I don't have any excuses for that, for her. I just don't want you to hate Kaia for some reason." And Ryker didn't even know why. He was just as angry at her right now.

"I don't. I won't." Charlie glanced to where Honor was perched on the fence, entranced with the horses. "For her."

His tight lungs unwound. "Thanks. I don't know why it matters so much to me."

"It matters because despite our best efforts, you and I will never be *her*." She flipped up her sunglasses, her evergreen eyes sinking into him like hooks. "Can never replace her. Never make it all better. So yeah, I get it. If my brother was a mess..." She winced. "Sorry."

"It's okay. She is a mess. I'm not denying that by any means."

"I'd defend him, too."

The impromptu drive with Ryker last night had gone unexpectedly well. When Honor had actually used words to ask if her uncle could come with them for a convertible ride, Charlie had barely resisted stomping her foot and throwing a tantrum. Instead, she'd figuratively put on her big-girl britches and invited him.

After, Honor had gone to sleep contentedly, her ratty bunny clutched against her pink-and-purple-striped pajamas. No matter what Charlie washed the bunny in, it stayed in its Velveteen Rabbit state. It might not look clean, but it was as good as it would get.

She peeked out the back door of the shop, which she'd left open as she worked on replacing a mass airflow sensor. She'd already cleaned it and cleared the codes, but the sensor must be bad, since it had popped back up as a problem.

Honor was in the sandbox again. Charlie had purchased a few new toys for it, including a miniature dump truck and some buckets for building castles.

She listened for sounds of Honor needing her as she worked. Ryker was due over soon for another visitation, and Charlie didn't have time to supervise another park expedition. She'd always known it would be a push to do the single foster mom thing, but she hadn't realized how behind she'd get at work. She'd had a customer leave to go to the other mechanic in town this morning when she'd told him it would be two days before she could get to his catalytic converter.

That killed her. She had to figure out a way to balance Honor and work. And she hadn't been over to the café next door to check on the demolition, either. She had seen the crew going in and out today, though, so she was thankful things were developing, even if she didn't know what they were.

Scrambling to catch up wasn't at all her normal mode of operation.

"Hello, anybody here?" Ryker poked his head inside the back door of the shop.

"I'm here." She peeled herself out from under the hood. "Sorry. Just finishing up."

"No problem." He stared at her for a beat too long, making Charlie question her appearance. She wore coveralls and had a bandanna holding back her short red locks. Nothing bothered her like her hair getting in the way while she was working.

"Listen, I—"

"Do you need us to stay here so you can finish up and supervise the visitation at the same time?"

She'd just been about to ask him for exactly that. Her jaw swung low. "Ah, yeah. That would be great, if you don't mind. Honor's been learning to ride without training wheels. Her bike's in the garage in the alley."

"I didn't realize she brought a bike with her."

"She…didn't." A bike wasn't that expensive, and it had made Honor's whole face light up. She'd practically wiggled with excitement when Charlie had showed it to her. She'd do the same a hundred more times for the same results.

Ryker's head quirked as if he was trying to solve an algebra equation. "All right. We'll be out here."

As she installed the new sensor, Charlie listened to the sound of Ryker coaching and encouraging Honor. The girl must have fallen off the bike, because there was a small bout of crying, which turned to giggles in a matter of seconds.

Ryker let out a big cheer as Charlie unbolted the casing covering the air filter. Honor must have gotten in a good run. After replacing the filter, which would hopefully help the sensor to last longer, Charlie cleaned up in the shop bathroom that was just outside the small front office. She tossed her gloves and hung her coveralls on a hook. She'd worn a soft heather-gray vintage T-shirt tonight and cuffed jean shorts, assuming she'd have to jump from working to supervising Ryker's visit. After washing up, she dried her hands and pumped lemon lotion onto her palm, rubbing it up to her elbows.

Outside, she found Ryker and Honor had switched over to the sandbox. They'd built a castle that stretched around the outside and were designing a river in the middle.

He really is a good guy.

Charlie didn't want to admit it. The selfish part of her wanted Ryker to be a deadbeat uncle, to scram and not show up. Instead he was moving to Colorado in order to expedite the process of becoming Honor's caregiver. He loved his sister but didn't defend her actions. He was… not what she'd expected. Especially after their first encounter at the park.

"Who's up for a snack?"

"Me!" Honor popped up from her perch on the side of the sandbox, a dust storm dropping from her clothes as she did.

Charlie went over and brushed as much as she could from her, emptying the cuffs of her shorts. "You coming up?" she questioned Ryker.

His chest rocked back. "Am I…" She thought he was going to say *wanted*, but he went with "welcome?" instead.

Wanted. Such a loaded word. Charlie had noticed Ryker, of course, but she hadn't allowed herself to sway in the attraction direction, because he was Honor's uncle. The person who would take the girl from her, most likely. And even now, she didn't know how to trust if what he said or did was true. He could be putting on a show to get closer to Honor. Pretending to be this man.

Charlie didn't think that was true, but how could she know? She'd never been very good with male relationships. She'd had guy friends, sure. Plenty of them with all of the mechanical classes she'd taken. But her dating experiences were very limited.

The one time she'd been asked out in high school,

she'd thought it was her first date. Turned out it was a guy trying to get another girl's attention, using her as bait. It had worked. They'd started dating shortly after. And once, Charlie had put the nail in her own coffin. She'd had a crush on a guy she'd considered a good friend. She'd asked him out, and it had ruined everything, because he hadn't been interested in her romantically. Their friendship had quickly faded to nonexistent.

To say she was terrible at reading men would be the understatement of the century.

The experiences had soured Charlie's taste for relationships and driven home that while she could rebuild a 1967 Mustang convertible with her granddad, she didn't have the same knack of understanding when it came to the male species.

How did a person ever fully know who someone else was?

"Yes, you're welcome to come up with us." Charlie was going to go with her gut about Ryker until something proved her wrong. And so far, he'd done nothing but show up for Honor and love on the girl. He hadn't raised his voice once since the park. She hadn't glimpsed even an iota of the man from that first night.

"Okay. I'd like that. Thanks."

Honor slipped her little hand into Charlie's as they walked up the wooden stairs that led to their apartment above the auto shop. "Do you want some milk, too, Uncle Ryker?" She glanced back at him.

"How else am I going to grow strong bones and teeth?"

His quip made Charlie's mouth quirk. *Strong* was definitely a word she'd use to describe the man, though it looked as if he stayed in shape from physical labor and not necessarily the gym.

Noticing him isn't a crime. At least that's what Charlie told herself. But believing that noticing him would amount to anything definitely was.

Ryker and Honor sat on stools at the breakfast bar, and Charlie served up milk for the little girl.

"What can I get you to drink? I've got iced tea and water."

"Milk would be great." He winked as if they were in cahoots somehow, and Charlie's chest gave a tug. She hadn't expected to like Ryker Hayes in any way, shape or form, but he was growing on her.

Charlie sliced an apple and put out a bowl of animal crackers. They'd eaten dinner earlier—chicken nuggets, because she hadn't had time for anything else. It had been Honor's favorite meal so far based on the way she'd snatched them up. Before Honor had gone from idea to reality, Charlie had planned to feed her future foster kiddo fruits and vegetables and only the healthiest of meals. Now, she was just happy when Honor ate something. Anything.

"Tell me about school." Ryker bit the head off a giraffe cracker and then imitated it crying in pain.

Honor giggled and then chomped on a tiger herself. "It's good."

"What's your favorite part?"

"Singing songs." She danced a bear cracker across the countertop. "I'm going to be in a play."

Ryker glanced at Charlie, questions written in the pucker of his brow. She shrugged in silent answer. She didn't know what Honor was talking about.

"What play, Hon?"

"The school play. I'm going to be Carmony Candy."

Their concerned gazes collided for a second time. Charlie leaned against the countertop, lowering herself to Honor's level. "Did your school send home something about this?"

Honor nodded and hopped down. She returned with a crumpled piece of paper that looked as if it had been stuffed in the bottom of a backpack.

Sure enough, the meeting about the play was tomorrow night. The sheet said that all kids who wanted to take part in the play had to attend the meeting with a parent. If they missed it, they wouldn't be allowed to try out for a part.

"Guess I'm going to a meeting about a play." Hyperventilating wasn't really her thing, but Charlie was considering it. How was she going to get everything done?

Divide and conquer. You can do this. Somehow.

Tonight she'd make a list of her to-dos, and then she'd tackle the items based on their importance. Charlie met things head-on—conversations and problems—whenever possible. But she'd also only ever had to watch out for and take care of herself. Adding a five-year-old into the mix was definitely shaking things up.

"Can I see?" Ryker reached for the paper, which Charlie handed over. He scanned the sheet. "Guess *we'd* better go to this meeting." It didn't come out as a question, because it wasn't for him.

Charlie wasn't fighting the urge to slug Ryker anymore, and she could see his good qualities, but she wasn't ready to coparent, either. And yet, what could she do about that? Like it or not, Ryker was in Honor's life now—and by association, Charlie's, too.

They were both vested in the girl, which meant Charlie would have to get over spending time with Ryker and realize that each of them was focused on Honor. She was all that mattered. Even if Charlie lost her to Ryker in the end—which, if he followed through on Angela's requirements, she probably would—she had to do what was right for Honor.

"For Honor's sake?" She raised eyebrows at Ryker. It was a question, a challenge. The only arrangement that made sense. And if Honor wasn't in the room with them, Charlie would state her intent more clearly.

Ryker gave a firm nod, as if understanding the implications behind the brief expression. "For Honor's sake."

At least they agreed on something.

Chapter Four

Ryker had called every ranch within a thirty-mile radius of Westbend. No one was hiring. He'd even contacted the horse ranch that they'd driven by the other night and left a message. It was a long shot. He certainly wouldn't be holding his breath while waiting for Sunny Farms to call him back.

He was about to start marching door to door in town looking for work. He'd seen a construction crew demoing the place next to Charlie's Garage. He could go by there and check if they needed an extra man. Ryker didn't have construction experience, but he was willing to do anything for Honor.

Which was why he was about to walk into a meeting about an elementary play. Would his sister have gone to this thing? Doubtful. And yet Charlie, who was running a business and basically volunteering to care for her, would.

Ryker could no longer deny Charlie's value in Honor's life. He just wasn't sure how she fit into the long-term picture. If it was up to him, he'd earn the right to raise

Honor. Until his sister reappeared and regained custody… or lost Honor for good.

The thought made him sick. How had Kaia gotten so off course? Ryker had tried various ways of getting in contact with her, but every attempt he'd made became a dead end. Her voice mail was full—because of his messages, most likely—and she didn't answer his texts. What if she never came back? What if having Honor taken from her was a ticket to freedom in her mind? Ryker was desperate to hear from her, to know what she was thinking.

And if she did respond to him, he'd do his best not to shout and rage, because man, he was mad at her. Who left a kid in the dust? And before Kaia had even skedaddled, Honor had been fending for herself. Ryker had learned more from Angela about how the school had reported her for possible neglect because of so many absences in just a few weeks of school. She'd also been without lunch on numerous occasions. And that was outside of the fact that she wore the same clothes to school on repeat, without even the illusion of a shower or bath.

The whole thing made him want to kick something and then empty the contents of his stomach.

A pair of small arms wrapped around his legs, and he glanced down. Sweet Honor peered up at him.

"Did you hear her?" Charlie asked from two steps behind. She wore ankle-length jeans and a simple white T-shirt with her leather sandals. Casual. Distracting. Just like when he'd poked his head into the back of her shop last night and found himself tongue-tied. She'd had a bandanna holding back her bright red locks, and all of the focus had been on those smoky green eyes of hers.

"No, sorry."

"She called out to you as we were walking in your direction."

He hugged Honor. "I missed that. Sorry, kiddo. My mind was elsewhere."

The sun stretched toward the mountains as they walked into the elementary building together. Freshly scrubbed floors reflected fluorescent lights, and hooks along the walls were labeled for backpacks with shelves above.

"You excited about this play, Hon?"

Her head bobbed, and she chewed on a fingernail. They were down to nubs. The stress from her current situation had to come out somewhere.

Parents and students filled the brightly decorated classroom, sitting in folding chairs around the sides and back. The three of them found seats, though the only chairs left were the little ones at the desks that the students used.

Ryker pretended to fall out of the tiny chair, making Honor giggle, though it wasn't far from the truth. He barely fit in the thing, and he wasn't the tallest of men at five foot ten. His father was over six feet, but Ryker had taken after his mother in the height department. He'd bulked up in high school as a defense mechanism—as if his physical strength could squash the turmoil and verbal wake from his childhood. Now, his workout was the ranch. It kept him in shape, and the manual labor helped him crash at night. If only he could find another ranch to hire him so that he could stay in town.

Ryker shot up a desperate prayer request yet again. He'd said plenty of those lately.

"Thank you for being here." A woman with trendy black-framed glasses and a flowered dress began the meeting. She introduced herself as Ms. Rana—the play director—and went on to inform the group that each family would be called on to fill a volunteer spot.

Charlie bit her lip next to him, broadcasting some sort of upset. Ryker had two nervous nellies on his hands tonight.

Ms. Rana talked about the various roles available and the tryouts she would hold. Papers were stationed around the room with descriptions for various parts and explanations of other options for involvement, like the narrator and backstage crew, plus a group that would do a dance number. Ryker poked Honor at that. She'd always loved dancing.

Once everything had been outlined, Ms. Rana dismissed the group to check out parts and sign up for ones they were interested in trying out for. Kids were supposed to rank their top three choices, and parents were supposed to sign up on one of the volunteer sheets.

Three little girls who looked to be around Honor's age ran up to each other, discussing what parts they wanted. Honor nibbled on what was left of her right pinkie nail.

Did she have any friends?

Ryker's heart rolled up into his throat, making him nauseous all over again. Honor had probably cemented herself as the oddball the moment she'd come to school without any of the necessities. When she'd worn the same outfit on repeat or her hair hadn't been brushed.

What Ryker wouldn't do to get ahold of his sister right about now.

He scooped Honor into his lap, praying the chair would support them, praying for healing for Honor. "What do you want to sign up for, Hon?"

Charlie must have recognized his attempt to protect Honor, because she wore relief like another woman might douse herself in perfume or layers of makeup.

"Do you have any ideas of what parts you're interested in?" Charlie asked. "Or should we walk around and look at the sheets Ms. Rana set out?"

Honor paused from demolishing her fingernail. "I want to be Carmony Candy."

Ryker reached back in his mind. Hadn't that been one of the lead roles? There were five or six that would be on stage for most of the play according to Ms. Rana.

"I think they save parts like that for the older grades." Charlie shot him a panicked glance. *Ah.* So, it was one of the lead roles. "Why don't you scoot around the room and look at some of the other options? Then we can decide."

"Okay." A sad Honor pushed from his lap and shuffled to the first character photo, scanning the sheet.

"We can't let her try out for a spot like that, can we?" Charlie held her head in her hands, elbows propped on the short table, her voice muffled. "She'll never get it, and I just don't know if she can handle another blow right now." Her forearms crashed to the faux wood. "I mean, she barely talks. She's getting better, yes, but she's not some exuberant theatrical kid."

"I guess. I'm not sure what to do." Was he supposed to have answers? All he wanted was for Honor to be healthy and happy and safe. He'd prefer to pluck her out of kindergarten, give her a year to get settled, and then start over.

But that would have its repercussions, too.

He was starting to wonder if he should be here at

all or if Charlie was the better option for Honor. Who was he to think he knew anything about raising a kid?

"What about this one?" Charlie pointed out a part that had five lines. It wasn't the biggest role. Not the smallest, either. "It says the costume is pink." So far pink had been high on Honor's like list.

Honor's head swung from side to side.

"Okay, no problem." Though they were halfway through the sheets in the room at this point. No reason to panic. They'd figure something out that was a fit. Wouldn't they? Charlie wasn't trying to discourage Honor. She was simply directing her to roles she was more likely to get. Ones she'd be able to handle memorizing. It only made sense to be logical about the whole thing, didn't it? And protecting her at this point in her tumultuous life had to be a good thing.

"What about this?" Ryker indicated a sheet that showed a group dance. "You love to dance. You'd be great at this."

Honor shook her head, and Charlie's stomach churned.

After three more sheets outlining parts that would make sense for Honor's size and abilities—and three more refusals—Charlie fisted her hands in order to prevent throwing them in the air in exasperation. If Honor didn't pick something she was interested in, she'd be assigned a spot. It would be better for her to have some choice in the matter.

Ryker's features were drawn tight, and he scrubbed a hand across the back of his neck. Seemed like neither of them knew what they were doing in this moment. Did all parents feel this sense of desperation? This terrible

I don't know how to fix this drop in their gut? If so, it was a wonder anyone ever signed up for the job.

Charlie had assumed parenting would come naturally to her because she'd wanted a child for so long, but if she made a tick mark for all the instances she'd already failed or botched things up, she'd be out of paper. Parenting—temporarily or not—was stressful. The smallest details—like this play—felt big. Despite the classes she'd taken and the things she'd read, Charlie wasn't equipped to deal with any of this. And that pressure didn't include the strain of keeping her business running and on track. When she'd heard Ms. Rana say that all parents were required to sign up to volunteer, she'd stifled a whimper. The school was only asking for one shift per family, but with the garage and the construction at the café, plus the medical, vision and dental appointments that Honor required, it would take a herculean effort to carve space in her schedule.

She'd figure out a way, though. Honor was worth it. If Charlie was going to be in this relationship, she was going to be all the way in. When she got home tonight, she'd continue tackling her to-do list one item at a time. Her granddad had always called her fiercely capable, and she wasn't going to stop believing that moniker now.

She could call her granddad when she left here, and he'd encourage her like he always did. Even at ninety-six years old he was sharp as a tack and full of wisdom. But Charlie felt the tug to handle this herself. With God, of course. Her granddad had poured into her enough over the years that she had the tools. She could tap into that and overcome this bump in the road.

And then after she'd call and tell him about it. He'd

love that. He'd always championed her strength and tenacity.

Ryker nudged her arm, his skin against hers warm and strange and not altogether unwelcome. "What's on your mind?" They followed Honor as she flitted to another sheet.

"Just processing my schedule and the volunteer portion of this."

"I can help."

His offer caused that heat she'd experienced a moment ago to chill. Honor was her responsibility, not his. At least, not his *yet*.

Charlie wished she could rewind and erase her admission. Ryker might not be the worst person on the planet like she'd originally thought. He might even be good for Honor. But that didn't mean Charlie had to open up to him.

Ryker might not be the enemy anymore, but that didn't make him a friend, either.

She'd been naive too many times in the past and had gotten burned. She wouldn't be making that mistake this time around. Any relationship she and Ryker formed was about Honor and nothing more.

"I appreciate that, but I'll figure it out."

"This is a lot, isn't it?" She'd expected him to fight back, not to extend an olive branch.

Some people had voiced opinions that Charlie shouldn't be fostering as a single woman, but Ryker, as far as she could tell, didn't harbor any concerns like that. She only heard respect in his tone, which made hers turn up a degree.

"It is a lot, but she's worth it. I don't have any regrets."

Gratitude claimed his features, turning them distracting in a flash. "Thank you for that. When I think about the places she could have ended up…" His head shook. "I appreciate you being her home."

For now.

Neither of them filled in the phrase. But for all intents and purposes, they were still on opposing sides of the fence. In the midst of fighting for Honor's well-being, they were ultimately fighting each other for the right to care for the little girl. Yes, Charlie knew Ryker wanted Honor, but was he the right place for her? Or could she possibly do better? Charlie's income was stable, and her feet were cemented in this town.

Questions about what was best for Honor kept her awake at night, which wasn't a help in running her garage. The other day she'd left an old gasket on an engine and had almost installed a new oil filter on top before realizing it. Huge rookie mistake that could have caused a loss in oil pressure and damage to her customer's engine.

Charlie had also tossed around the theory that she should back out of fostering Honor and let Ryker have her. He was family, after all. But according to Angela, that wasn't even an option until he could provide what his niece required in terms of a living arrangement.

Which meant Charlie had to stay in this right now.

Plus, who knew if Ryker would stick things out? It was possible he wouldn't find a job here or a way to transfer his life from Texas to Westbend. The moving expenses of his old place plus a new one would break even the most stable of households.

And the jury was still out on whether he harbored any of his sister's tendencies. It had only been a week since he'd roared into town. For all Charlie knew, he'd leave the same way, and Honor would be heartbroken all over again.

No, she definitely wasn't ready to hand over the fight regarding Honor. Not until God made it clear that she should let go in the same way He'd shown her to commit in the first place.

"I really don't mind signing up for the volunteer spot. It's only one shift per family, so I can cover it."

Family. They were anything but that.

"I'd like to help if I can swing it."

"All right. Then I'll sign up for now, and if it works, you can later."

The weight bearing down on her eased a bit. "Okay. Thanks." Letting him fill in for the volunteer slot wasn't handing over Honor. As long as this wasn't just a way for Ryker to worm his way into proving something to Angela. Charlie internally cringed. It was tough not to doubt his intentions.

Honor finished perusing the sheets and then turned to face the two of them.

She spoke clearly, concisely. "I want to be Carmony Candy."

Charlie suppressed a groan. The last thing Honor needed was to reach for the stars and have her legs taken out from underneath her.

She kept her voice quiet, so that others wouldn't overhear, and soft, so that *she* didn't break Honor. "I don't think that's a—"

"Okay, Hon, if that's what you want to do, then you should try."

Charlie choked on a breath, fire and rage igniting at Ryker's interruption. He shouldn't even be here with them. Charlie had been willing to let him because she'd thought it was good for Honor—and had cleared it with Angela. But he was pushing his way in where he wasn't welcome.

"Yay!" Honor cheered and hugged Ryker, looping her arms around his knees.

Charlie wanted to shout, stomp her foot, scream. When Honor got hurt, she'd be the one figuring out how to comfort her. When she cried herself to sleep— as she had the first few nights—Ryker would be off somewhere, oblivious to what he'd done.

The man should come with a muzzle.

Good thing Charlie still had her barriers up when it came to Ryker, because otherwise, she'd have to start rebuilding.

Chapter Five

After Honor added her name to the tryout sheet for Carmony Candy and refused to put down second or third choices, Charlie snagged her hand and headed for the door while Ryker was otherwise occupied talking with another parent in the classroom.

If he wasn't currently cemented on her what-were-you-thinking naughty list, she might have waited for him, let him walk out with his niece. But her anger right now prevented that. Space would be a good thing. She had to calm down, process. And doing it without Ryker was better for everyone involved.

Outside, the sun had slipped behind the mountains, and bright pink and orange splashed through the sky like paint in a toddler's hands. The mountains never failed to remind her that God was present in her life. It was as if they shouted, *If God can do this, what can't He do?*

She got out her phone and sent a text to her friend Addie. Operation be-nice-to-uncle-for-Honor's-sake failing miserably. Send chocolate.

Addie's text reply came back quickly. What happened? Want company? Evan is here so I could pop over.

Charlie's strong burst of relief surprised her. She'd known fostering would be hard, but she hadn't expected the little details like tonight to leave her floundering and agitated. Wasn't she supposed to be fiercely capable?

Yes, please! We're still at school but should be home shortly.

Let me get Sawyer down for the night and then I'll text you before I leave to make sure you're home.

Perfect.

Addie had moved to town last spring to reopen the Little Red Hen Bed & Breakfast, and the two of them had quickly bonded. She had an adorable two-year-old son, Sawyer, and she'd recently become engaged to Evan Hawke. Charlie often hung out with the two of them. As couples went, they were pretty good at not making her feel like a third wheel, though the looks they exchanged when they assumed no one was paying attention required a fire extinguisher. They were planning their wedding for the first weekend in January, and Charlie was going to be a bridesmaid. She was happy for her friend and, most of the time, not jealous.

Most of the time.

But on a night like tonight, when the water was slipping over her head and her arms were tired of treading, she craved what the two of them had. What the three of them had.

They were a team. And Charlie—despite her willingness to participate in a relationship—was still a one-woman show. God was with her always, she knew that.

But having someone physically present who could hold her hand or pull her out of the raging waters when she got dumped overboard…yeah, she'd take one of those.

And if he had a baby in his arms…she'd take one of those, too.

When Charlie had turned thirty, she'd asked God for one thing—a child. It had been a crazy wish on so many levels, but she'd confessed her deepest desire and then tried her best to let go of it. To let God handle it. That's when God had planted the fostering dream inside her, and she'd latched on. Tentatively, yet cautiously optimistic.

There'd been a moment after she'd gotten the call about Honor when she'd let her mind wander down the what-if road. What if her mom's parental rights were eventually revoked? Would Charlie consider adopting Honor on her own? What would that look like? And would it fill that void inside her? Those musings had quickly crashed and burned once she'd learned that it was Kaia's first brush with losing custody *and* once Ryker had screeched into town.

"Hi, Honor." They were walking to the car along the fence that lined the school playground when a little girl with stunning chocolate eyes and equally dark hair swept into a braid stopped in front of them. "Do you want to play on the playground with me?"

Honor froze. After two beats, she glanced up at Charlie in silent question. "You can go play for a few minutes. I'll wait for you."

They scampered off, and Charlie's heart expanded three sizes. None of the kids in the meeting had spoken to Honor. Charlie had assumed the girl had very few friends, if any, and it had broken her heart for the sweet child.

"Charlie!" She turned at the sound of her name. One of the women she'd seen in the classroom came in her direction. "Hey, I'm Camila. Gabby's mom. I've brought my car in for service before." A faint Spanish accent peppered her introduction. The woman was gorgeous with her raven hair and olive skin.

"Right. I'm so sorry. Sometimes when I'm out of context—"

"Same thing happens to me all of the time." Camila waved her hand in a *don't worry about it* gesture. "I didn't realize you had a child at the elementary."

"I'm actually…here with Honor Delaney." Charlie pointed to the playground, where the two little girls were running across a balance beam.

"Oh, that's wonderful. That's my daughter, Gabby, right there. They must be friends. How sweet."

Or they're new friends, and your daughter is a gift sent from God.

"Anyway, I'm sorry to talk shop, but I've been meaning to bring my SUV in. I just can't seem to find the time."

"Tell me about it." Charlie silently chuckled at her inside joke, since she could hardly find the time to shower these days. She'd seemingly entered the newborn mom phase…with a five-year-old. "So, what's going on with your vehicle?"

"It's shifting strange. Kind of almost…jerking."

"Okay, well, it's best if you can drop it off sometime and I can drive it. How about Friday morning?" Charlie would block off a chunk in her schedule. Especially since Gabby was her new favorite person. The girls were swinging now, and the sound of their giggles about made Charlie weep with gratitude.

Honor never talked about anyone from school. Charlie would guess that was about to change. Sometimes all it took was one person to alter the course of a life. Her granddad had been that person for her. Maybe Honor would look back someday and remember the night Gabby had asked her to play.

Or maybe Charlie was long gone down a sappy road and needed to rein it in.

"Friday's great. I'll plan on leaving it in the morning. Thank you." Camila's phone rang, and she checked the screen. "My husband!" Her delight was palpable. "He's deployed, so his phone calls are like gold."

"That's so great! I'll hang out with the girls while you talk to him."

"Really? Thank you so much!" Camila greeted her husband as she walked to her vehicle and opened the driver's door, sitting inside for privacy.

Charlie sent a text to Addie explaining that they were going to hang out at the playground for a bit. She didn't know how long Camila's phone call would last, but the extra playtime wouldn't hurt. Maybe it would help Honor expend all her energy and sleep peacefully. Something Charlie prayed for her every night.

"This is the best sight I've seen since I arrived in Colorado." Ryker approached and motioned to the girls playing, his voice warm like caramel sauce melting ice cream. Charlie had never despised dessert to this level.

"You're still here? I thought you'd left."

"You wish, huh?" His low chuckle made her stomach flip and flop. That's what anger did to her digestive tract. "I'm still here. And I'm going to go out on a limb and say you're still upset with me."

"You reneged on the plan." So much for taking some

time to cool down. Charlie had just jumped right in. But she wasn't good at hiding her emotions—didn't have any practice at it. She was usually straightforward and drama-free. She was still the first, it seemed, but Ryker was tipping her scales regarding the second.

Ryker moved to the bench that flanked the fence and plunked down, his torso hunching over his knees like he'd been punched in the gut. And Charlie hadn't even entertained the thought…this time. At least, not for long.

"You're the one who came up with that idea in the first place. I wasn't sure what I thought about all of it. I just want what's best for Honor."

"I do, too! And you've obviously made your opinion clear. And now I'm going to have to deal with the repercussions of what you decided in the heat of the moment."

"Because you're in this all alone." Ryker radiated with a deadly, boiling heat.

"Yes, I am. As of this point, *I'm* Honor's caregiver. You still have hoops to jump through, and who knows if you actually will. You're here because I'm being gracious and talked to Angela about you attending this meeting. It's not like you even have a place for her." Charlie pulled back the arrow, unable to resist the urge to let it fly. "Or a job here. Who's to say everything doesn't fall through?"

"Ouch." Ryker sat back against the bench. "Tell me how you really feel." He raked hands through his hair. "Family first is supposed to be the motto, but they sure make it hard."

Charlie's empathy flared. Ryker was trying. She was just angry about the ambush in the school. If Honor were her niece, she'd do absolutely anything to take care of her.

Anything.

She had to find a way to balance caring for Honor and growing to love her with knowing she might have to hand her over to this man. Or someone else, even. There were so many unanswered questions that she was stumbling on repeat.

Honor's giggle broke the quiet. It was the kind of laugh that came from deep inside, that had to find a way out. She started to run to the slide, then stopped and reached back. Gabby grabbed her hand and they raced forward together.

Charlie's heart flat stopped. She might be terrified of what came next, but that little glimpse was the reminder that she was exactly where she was supposed to be.

"Thank you for stating my every fear into existence." Ryker's stony glare cut through the night in front of him, and the playground lights clicked on as if in answer, emitting a buzz. "And you just might get your wish, because I can't find a job." So much pain laced the admission that Charlie winced. She'd thought the idea of Ryker leaving town would bring her joy and relief.

Turns out, it didn't.

Remorse for the verbal onslaught Charlie had just lobbed his way overtook her features and surprisingly tugged on his sympathy.

How many times had Ryker done or said something and then instantly regretted it?

He certainly felt that way about the park fiasco last week.

"Sorry." Charlie's demeanor softened around the edges. "I'm not gunning for you to leave town. You're good for Honor. I'm not denying that. I'm just angry about what happened inside because she'll be crushed if she doesn't get the part, and I'm not sure *I* can handle watching her go through that. She's already weathered enough."

"I understand. And I deserve the backlash for blindsiding you like that."

Charlie moved toward the bench, taking a seat next to him. *Next* meaning she'd left a foot of space between them. Was it strange that Ryker wished she'd sat closer? That way he could inhale lemons and Charlie. That way he wouldn't feel so alone in all of this.

Yes, Hayes, it's strange. She's not on your team. At least not fully. Ryker wasn't even sure he could call her a friend at this point. This whole situation fighting for Honor was so messed up. Normally Ryker got along with pretty much everyone. But for how amiable Charlie seemed to be, she had some walls up. She was protecting herself, and Ryker didn't blame her.

Honor and her new friend had climbed up a tower on the playground, and their heads bent together as they discussed something. They giggled, screeched and ran across a wooden bridge that connected the equipment.

"I didn't tell Honor to go for the part because I'm trying to ruin anything for her or you. I just…" Her little face had been so hopeful that Ryker hadn't wanted to erase that. "She's already had so many disappointments in her life. Has likely been told she's not good enough— verbally or nonverbally—by people or society on numerous occasions. I just wanted to believe in her, with her. If Honor wants to dream big when she's probably never done that before and we're here to help her—"

"And catch her," Charlie interjected with a sigh.

"Right. And catch her. If she wants to go for it, I can't

be the one to tell her no before she's even tried. I'm sorry for backing out of the plan." *The plan you came up with and I never actually agreed to.* Thankfully he didn't let that bomb fly.

"I get that. I do. It's just… Carmony Candy is a big part, which the director said would likely go to one of the older kids. She doesn't even fit the description for the character in size or age. Feels like setting her up to fail."

"Yeah. I just thought—or hoped—that hearing it from the director, letting her handle it, was better than us crushing the idea before she tried. I know it's not the same, but what if someone had told you that you couldn't be a mechanic because you're a girl?"

Charlie snorted. "Plenty of people told me that."

"Well, then it only made you stronger. But how nice would it have been if someone believed in you?"

Charlie waited a few beats, then answered quietly. "Someone did. My granddad. My parents are great, but he was the one who really saw me and always, always encouraged me. He was an airplane mechanic in World War II."

"An older couple that lived near us, they did that for me. They believed in me. Let me work with horses at their ranch. They changed my life." The Armijos had welcomed him into their ranch and their home for dinner on more occasions than Ryker could count. They'd talked about God, and he'd believed because they'd lived it. "So we have to let her fly a little. Not too far. Not over a cliff. Just let her dream and try, I think. Just like we both needed."

"Don't tell me what to do." Charlie coupled the statement with a grin, and Ryker chuckled.

"I wouldn't dare."

"You just did dare."

"Yeah, but I'm right."

Charlie wrinkled her nose. "I'm not so sure about that, and even if I was…" Her sassy smile registered like a hoof to his gut. "I would never admit it."

Fine by him. Ryker had a few things he never planned to admit, either. Like the fact that Charlie intrigued him more every day. It was too bad they hadn't met outside of this situation. But with Honor between them, letting anything grow in that regard would be hazardous. Too much could go wrong. Too much was up in the air. And Ryker *had* to focus on his niece. He couldn't get distracted, and he refused to repeat his mother's mistakes. She'd allowed her romantic relationships to come first, even before her children, and Ryker and Kaia had suffered on repeat because of it.

"So, what's the dealio with the job hunt?"

Ryker wasn't sure if he should spill everything to Charlie about his job-search issues, but at this point, he had nothing to lose by sharing.

"I'm not sure. I've called around pretty much everywhere I can find, and no one is hiring."

"And you were a ranch hand in Texas?"

"Yep." Compared to Charlie's success, Ryker was nothing. He might have been dependable and good at what he did, but when he saw all the irons she had in the fire—her mechanic shop and the place she was planning to open next door—he was as successful as a beetle on its back in the middle of a massive lake.

"There are so many ranches around here."

"You know of any that are hiring?"

"Not offhand. But I could ask my friend Addie. Her fiancé has some connections to Wilder Ranch."

"I stopped by there, and they said at the beginning of the season they would have had openings, but not going into fall. They're slimming down staff at this point."

"Yeah, that makes sense. So maybe you have to make a change of some sort. If you could do anything, what would you do?"

"Find a job. *Any* job."

"I get that, but..." Charlie inched closer. "What's your dream? You can't hide it after you forced us to let Honor go for hers."

True. "I'd like to work with horses and teens, because horses are what saved me when I was a kid, but I have no idea how to make that happen. It's a pointless dream if it's impossible."

"Dreams are never pointless." Charlie snapped her fingers. "What about that horse ranch that we drove by the other night?"

"Sunny Farms. I called there."

"And?"

"I left a message about looking for work. No one called me back."

Charlie's expression shot straight to incredulous. "And that's it? You're just going to leave it at that? Why aren't you driving out there? Following up?" A car door shut behind them. "That's Camila—Gabby's mom. She had to take a phone call."

Perfect timing. Ryker didn't want to get into this conversation with anyone, let alone Charlie—the woman far more successful than him and therefore likely more qualified to take care of his niece than he was.

"So you're going to push Honor to dream big, but

you won't do the same with yourself? Is that what I'm hearing?"

Charlie didn't understand. She'd grown up differently than he had. She hadn't been emotionally—and sometimes physically—kicked around by her mom's boyfriends until she no longer remembered who she was or what she was capable of.

That was his story, not hers. "You don't get it."

"You're right. I don't. And based on the fact that I'm growing attached to Honor, I'm probably the last person who should be telling you this, but don't give me a sob story about how you've done everything you can to find a job when you haven't. You're saying that Sunny Farms would be your first choice, and you haven't even driven out there. Sounds like self-sabotage to me."

It did.

Ryker had stopped by some other ranches, but not the one highest on his interest list. He was dragging his boots regarding Sunny Farms. It was just…he wasn't trained in anything they would need. Yes, he'd worked with horses in high school for the Armijos and after at the Circle M, but that likely wouldn't be enough. Sunny Farms hadn't called him back, had they?

You'll never amount to nothing. Take out the trash, including yourself.

Ever since he'd arrived in Colorado, sending his life into upheaval, the insults from his childhood had played through his mind like an endlessly skipping CD. Ryker tried to combat the lies with Bible verses and prayers, but the taunts had staying power.

Camila rounded the fence and called out for her daughter. She still had the phone pressed against her

To:
Prince Albert - John M. Cuelenaere

IN-TRANSIT

From: zcr
Date: Monday, Jul 12 2021 3:03PM

Title: Raising Honor
Material type: Book
Call number: PB LYN
Item barcode: 33292300078478
Assigned branch: Prince Albert - John M. Cuelenaere

ear. "Come, honey, Daddy wants to say hi to you." She waved at Charlie. "Thank you so much!"

The girls began their descent from the playground equipment. "All I'm saying—" Charlie rushed to impart her final blow, lowering her voice "—is that you made Honor dream, so maybe you should do the same."

"Why are you helping me?"

Her eyes flashed with remorse and confusion, her response a whisper. "I really don't know. I just want what's best for Honor."

Me, too. But if he believed everything that had been pounded into him growing up…he wasn't good enough for his niece.

Wasn't good enough for anyone.

No wonder he couldn't find a job. Why would someone else believe in him when he couldn't believe in himself?

Chapter Six

"Can I ride the bus to school this morning?"

Honor's question instantly changed Charlie's trajectory. She'd been heading for a coffee refill. Instead she came to a screeching halt next to the breakfast bar where Honor was shoving her lunch box into her backpack.

"How come you want to ride the bus this morning?" Charlie had been driving her since her arrival. It felt like old habit now. Changing things might sting...a lot.

A shrug answered.

"Is there a friend you want to ride with?"

Honor shook her head.

"You just want to try it out, huh?"

A nod answered.

Okay. Charlie inhaled, exhaled. "I mean, yeah, sure, I guess. If that's what you want to do."

Honor flashed a winning smile that Charlie took as confirmation that she was doing the right thing. Angela had said from the start that Honor could ride the bus. Charlie was the one who hadn't been ready yet.

After finishing their morning routine, they headed for the bus stop.

At the edge of the garage lot, Honor paused. "I'll go by myself."

"Are you—" Charlie didn't get to finish her question. Honor had already joined the group of kids converging on the bus stop from various directions.

The pickup location was one block away, but the distance might as well be a mile for how far it felt.

Charlie waited for the bus to appear, sipping from her coffee mug, acting as if this was normal everyday stuff when it was actually huge, never-happened-before stuff.

When the bus pulled up and the door swung open, Honor hopped on without a glance back. A good thing, Charlie reminded herself as she entered the shop, donned her coveralls and popped in her earbuds. Maybe a little independence could be good for both of them.

First on her docket today was replacing an alternator. The procedure soothed her as she disconnected cables and the heat shield, removed the drive belt. She hummed along to her country playlist while she worked.

Charlie was usually pretty put together. Organized. Liked to know what was happening and when and why. She enjoyed math and logic and things that made sense—like engines. She wasn't a fan of game playing or emotional drama.

Yet ever since Honor had entered her life along with her uncle, all of the structure Charlie craved had flown out the window. Since working on her to-do lists the last few nights after Honor went to bed, she finally felt as if she'd found her rhythm again.

Between songs on her playlist, she heard the back door of the shop open. She turned to greet Scott.

"Morning."

Except the figure inside the door was taller and

broader than the young mechanic. Charlie let out a screech of recognition and flew over to her brother. "What are you doing here?" She hugged him, making sure her gloves didn't land on any of his clothes, and he laughed, squeezing her back.

"I finally found the one." Finn wore a checked button-down shirt, jeans and boots. His long legs had always made her jealous, since Charlie clocked in at five foot six.

"A woman?"

"Definitely not one of those. At least, not again." Charlie knew Finn had been involved with a woman for a short stint of time, but things hadn't ended well, and Finn had been mum on the details. "A ranch. I'm buying the Burkes' place. Finally found the right amount of land, right setup."

Charlie removed her gloves. "That's so great. Come grab a cup of coffee with me. Tell me about it." They went into the office, and she brewed a new pot while her brother told her details about the number of acres, the house and outbuildings.

Finn took his coffee black, so Charlie filled a mug for him and handed it off before doctoring her own. "I'm so happy for you, brother. Congratulations." They clinked cups. "It's about time you got here. I moved here thinking you'd be here first, and now I'm the local."

Finn's grin showcased white teeth. Braces—with headgear, as Charlie happily recalled—had gotten him the perfect smile. There hadn't been much she could tease her little brother about and win, as he'd been bigger than her almost from the start, but she'd definitely bruised him up over the embarrassing headgear.

"I'm glad I finally found the right place with the right terms. Trust me, I wanted to be here a while ago."

"To escape a certain someone?"

Finn swirled the coffee in his mug, momentarily mesmerized by it. "That's not the reason why, as this was always my plan after leaving Wilder Ranch. Save money and get a place of my own." He met her gaze, hurt lurking in the shadows of his. "But the timing...yeah, I'm all right with that part."

If only he'd tell her the whole story. "I'm sorry it's been rough."

"Nothing to be sorry about." Darkness claimed his features for a second, but he shook it off. "So, what about you? How's the kid?"

"She's great. Still adjusting to everything, of course, but I can see her starting to relax, to feel safe." Her throat filled with a ball of emotion. "She didn't ask for any of the mess she's been dealt, that's for sure."

"You're doing a good thing, sis."

"Thanks." But that wasn't why she'd signed up. Caring for Honor wasn't about earning brownie points or jewels in her crown. She'd just...known this was her next thing. Her next to-do. Sort of like she'd known to open the last shop in Colorado Springs that she'd ended up selling, and then followed her gut to Westbend once Finn had planned to buy a ranch and settle nearby. "It's funny. She rode the bus to school this morning, and you would've thought she drove the car herself based on my reaction. I missed driving the tyke. She's not very chatty, but we're comfortable with each other." At least Charlie was comfortable with Honor. She couldn't speak for the girl's feelings.

"Huh."

Finn's lack of response grated. "What do you mean by that?"

He topped off his coffee. "Nothing."

"Finn Marshall Brightwood." His middle name had come from their granddad, and Charlie had often been jealous of that connection, too. Though if the old man was picking favorites…she had no doubt they'd both assume they were the golden child. Their dad's dad was a rock star in that way. "Spill."

He took his sweet time sipping coffee before acquiescing. "I just don't want you getting hurt. It's hard for me to hear you're getting attached when this sounds like it's going to be a short-term gig."

She'd bombarded Ryker the other night at school by spouting all of his fears, and now Finn was doing the same to her. "I know what I signed up for, and it's going to come with a certain amount of pain one way or the other. But I'd rather live and endure some hurt than hole up and hide."

Finn took that in slowly, digesting it as if it had something to do with him and not just her. His shoulders squared. "That makes sense. We have to keep living."

What in the world had his last relationship done to him? Finn was usually so strong, so positive. Willing to see and believe the best in everyone.

"If loving Honor brings me some pain…" She raised her cup as if to say *what can I do?* "It is what it is. I'm here now, and I'm not quitting."

"You sound like a Brightwood."

They shared a smile at their granddad's saying.

"I can't wait for you to meet Honor. Do you have time today?"

"I'll make time."

And that, Charlie thought, was why she'd missed her brother. So it was a good thing he was about to get his rear end back to Colorado. She could use some more of his balance and steadiness in her life.

During the last three days, Ryker had worked for Alma Dinnerson doing projects at her rental properties. While she hadn't offered him the duplex—unfortunately the showing after his had rented it without needing to delay the deposit—Alma had still rescued him by throwing him some work, even if it was only temporary. And she'd also referred him to a couple who rented out a room in their basement on a monthly basis.

It wasn't ideal—Ryker would have preferred to find a two-bedroom right away—but considering that he didn't have a permanent job and that he still owed rent for his room in Texas, Alma's solution was a godsend. The space had its own entrance but not a full kitchen, so he'd have to make do with a toaster oven and microwave, which wasn't really a hardship. He didn't cook much beyond using those appliances anyway, and the minifridge would work for him, too.

He'd been able to afford the month of rent they'd asked for, and they hadn't made him sign anything long-term, understanding that he'd be moving on quickly.

Ryker had moved his things over from the Lazy Bones Motel last night. He didn't have furniture, except for his army cot, which he'd thrown into the back of his truck at the last second before leaving Texas. He'd be sleeping on that for the foreseeable future. The couple had left a small table and two chairs in the room for him to borrow, so the setup would work fine. And now that he had a place to call his own, albeit small, he'd have one of his old roommates ship some more of his things.

While Ryker appreciated the work and room Alma had sent his way and her quick payment which would help him stay afloat, it was now early Friday afternoon, and he still hadn't found a permanent job that would allow him to stay in Colorado.

He couldn't ignore Charlie's challenge to him about Sunny Farms any longer. If he was going to fail at getting his dream job, he at least had to put forth a decent effort first.

Ryker popped back to his new place and showered, then dressed in jeans, boots and a button-down that hopefully screamed *cowboy* and *good with horses*. He forced himself into his truck, his foot hesitant on the pedal as he drove to Sunny Farms.

All they can do is say no, and I'm already at that juncture. It can't get worse than my current situation.

The jaded pep talk did little to encourage him. Hearing *no* from Sunny Farms would sting, no doubt. That's why he'd been avoiding driving out there all week.

He wound out of town, finding his way by memory. It was a beautiful spread, and as his truck kicked up dust down the long drive, he fought the strangest sense of rightness. *Wishful thinking.*

He parked and made his way over to a woman in an outdoor arena who was training young riders. After about fifteen minutes, the instructions ended. The kids led their horses to the stables along with another staffer, and the woman came Ryker's way.

"Afternoon," she called out. "Something I can help you with?"

Ryker sucked in a breath and shot up a silent prayer.

"I left a message a few days ago." He swallowed to combat the desert currently residing in his mouth. "Wondering if you're hiring."

The woman wore a Sunny Farms polo with jeans and boots. Ryker would place her in her midfifties. Her face bore faint wrinkles, but they were the variety that seemed to come from the sun and contentment.

"I'm Lou. Short for Louisa, but if you call me that, I won't answer." She offered her hand, and Ryker shook it. "Our phone system has been acting up. Not sure I heard your message, or I would have called you back. We just posted a job yesterday. What are you looking to do?"

Ryker's pulse thundered. "Anything."

By the time they finished talking thirty minutes later, Ryker had a job. A dream job. Because not only did the ranch raise and sell world-class horses, they offered an internship program to college students and employed teens as barn assistants. After his training, Lou wanted part of his job to be managing the teens.

If Ryker were a crying man, he'd seriously consider it.

Lou asked if he could start on Monday, so he filled out some paperwork before leaving. Shaky and surprised and grateful over how things had gone, Ryker got back in his truck and rumbled down the dirt drive.

"Guess I'm not as much of a screwup as you'd thought I would be, huh, Bruce?" He tossed the comment into the universe, hoping it smacked into the man who'd made it his mission to verbally kick Ryker on every occasion possible. Mom hadn't listened when Ryker had tried to explain how Bruce had treated him, so eventually, he'd stopped telling her. He'd figured out how to fend for himself. To get out of the house every chance he could get.

God had been waiting for him at the Armijos'. Ryker had healed a lot over the years, but when things got dicey, those old wounds reopened and festered.

Not anymore. Not in Colorado.

Crazy to think that a job that had hatched out of an emergency could actually be exactly where he was supposed to be.

Without Charlie challenging him, Ryker wouldn't have driven out to Sunny Farms. He wouldn't have found a position that made his pulse fly. And he wanted to tell her about it. Her and Honor.

It was time for school to let out. If he hurried, he could catch the girls at pickup and share his good news.

Despite the fact that he was working toward taking over Honor's care, he was strangely confident Charlie would celebrate with him—especially since she was the one who'd pushed him to apply in person.

Ryker slowed when he reached the school and scanned the pickup line out front. It was jammed with vehicles, so he pulled to the side of the road to get a better look. If he spotted them, he could throw his truck in Park and jog over, since space was limited.

Charlie's red Mustang was in the second aisle, three cars back. A man filled the passenger seat. Tall. Lean. Young—around his or Charlie's age. Ryker's gut fell through the floorboard of his truck. He'd thought she wasn't dating anyone. And even if it was just a friend, the last thing Honor needed in her life was some random guy.

The man got out to let Honor in the back seat and greeted her by bending to her level. She didn't hug him. After a short conversation that Ryker would give anything to hear, she hopped in the back and the three of them rolled away. He sat, staring out the windshield as the traffic eased and parents and children vacated the lot.

He couldn't decide if he was angry or hurt. Charlie was allowed to have a life, no doubt. But when it affected Honor...it became his business.

Charlie formed burger patties as Honor and Finn built a castle out of blocks in the living room. Since she no longer had space for Finn to stay at her apartment, he was renting a room at Little Red Hen Bed & Breakfast, which Addie ran. In an impromptu move, Charlie had invited Addie, Evan and Sawyer over for dinner tonight along with her brother.

With Finn showing up unexpectedly and she and Scott catching up at work today, this was the lightest Charlie had felt in a long time. She'd also checked on the progress of the construction next door and had been pleased to find that her contractor was on the ball and things were on schedule.

And even better than all of that—Honor had come home from school chatting about Gabby. The girls were quickly developing a close friendship, and each day Honor seemed more adjusted, less lost, more at peace. She'd even taken to Finn quickly. Though who wouldn't? Charlie's brother was the best of the best. As dependable and supportive as a summer day was long.

A knock sounded on her door, and then Addie poked her head inside. "It's us."

"Come in!"

"It's me, it's me." Sawyer marched into the apartment as if he was a king, and to Charlie, he was. She adored the little rascal.

"Hey, trouble." She quickly washed and dried her hands so that she could scoop the toddler up in a hug. "We got some new building blocks. That's my brother, Finn, playing with Honor. You should go check them out." The moment she released Sawyer, he did exactly that.

Charlie greeted Addie and Evan with hugs, then accepted the pan full of something delicious from her friend. "What did you bring me?"

"Strawberry shortcake."

Charlie's saliva glands kicked on full force. "Yum. You're my favorite friend ever."

Addie laughed. "Right back at ya."

Charlie made introductions between Finn and Evan from her perch in the kitchen. Addie had met her brother previously. A hum of conversation filled her apartment, and Charlie's heart expanded. This was good. Really good. For once she wasn't doubting her choice to provide a home for Honor. The girl's recent improvement was all the proof she needed.

"I'm going to throw these on the grill." She snagged the plate of patties. "Be right back." She headed down the outdoor wooden stairs. It was so bright with the sun beaming down at a slant that she almost didn't notice Ryker sitting in his pickup truck, parked in the alley.

Almost.

Charlie plunked the platter of meat on the metal shelf attached to the grill. "What are you doing over there?" She raised her voice so that Ryker would hear her through his half-open window. The man was the definition of a stalker, sitting in his truck unannounced like that. Her insides even gave a squeeze of recognition that something was off as he hopped out of his vehicle and came her way. It was the first time he'd displayed any action reminiscent of their heated run-in at the park.

Weird. Charlie ignored the tweak in her universe and started the grill. It would need to warm up a minute before she added the burgers.

Ryker leaned against the wooden staircase, facing her, not saying anything.

"What is going on with you?" Her arms crossed without her permission, but the chill accompanying the man required a sweater.

"I think the better question is, what's going on with you?" Ryker glanced away, almost broadcasting…hurt. But that didn't make any sense. Charlie hadn't seen him since the meeting at school on Tuesday night.

"Look, Ryker, I'm terrible at games, so spit it out. What's your deal?" Had he seen she was having people over? Was he upset he wasn't invited or something? No way. That option was too junior high to be possible.

"I went out to Sunny Farms this afternoon. They had a position and hired me on the spot."

"What? That's so great!" Charlie should be happy for him, right? She kept telling herself that Ryker getting his stuff in order was the best scenario for Honor. The girl should be with family. That's how the system worked. That's how things would likely end up. Charlie would figure out a way to adjust. To trust that God had a plan in all of it that she couldn't see yet. And to trust that if Honor ended up with Ryker, that's where she was supposed to be.

"Yeah. It was." Ryker's huff cut off further explanation.

"You still seem upset. I don't understand."

He shoved agitated hands into his jeans' pockets. "I

got the job and the only thing I could think about was telling Honor…and you."

Her pulse skipped and jumped rope. "Oh." That was nice. What did that mean?

"I went by school to tell you. It was on my way back into town. And what do I see but you picking up Honor with some guy in your car. I'm not sure who it is. Was. But I don't think she needs anyone influencing her right now who's not one of us. She's too vulnerable. And I know what it is to have a rotten male influence in my life. I don't want that for her."

He was at a ten on the volume meter.

"Are you done yet?" Charlie jerked open the metal grill cover and began shoving burgers onto the sizzling grate. "I don't appreciate the insinuation that I'd bring anyone questionable around Honor. You don't know me well enough to make accusations like that, Ryker Hayes."

"Well, I didn't know what to think when I rolled up and saw the three of you."

Steps sounded on the wooden platform above them. "Char? You all right down there? Evan thought he heard a commotion."

Ryker's face flipped to bright red, and he pointed above them as if to say *told you so*. As if proving she'd had a man with her in the car. *Please.* Charlie barely resisted poking the metal spatula into Ryker's chest.

"Yeah. I'm fine." She answered her brother, voice surprisingly smooth despite the anger heating through her. "Give me a minute, okay?"

Finn's hesitation sounded in his slow return inside. Finally, the door clicked shut. "You had better pull yourself together, Ryker, or you're going to repeat that first day in the park, and how far would that set you back? Coming over here to accuse me of something was a terrible idea. You can't just pop by whenever you get the whim. Pick up the phone and call me next time. Ask me straight out."

"That's what I'm trying to do."

"Well, you're doing an awful job of it." She finished adding the patties and slammed the lid down with excess force, causing a *clang* to reverberate through her arm. "And it's not like I have to explain my decisions to you."

"I know." The words exploded. "That's what makes it so hard." Ryker scrubbed fingers through his hair, leaving the disheveled locks in stark contrast to the rest of him. Smooth cheeks boasted a recent shave, and his long-sleeved button-down was coupled with crisp jeans.

He'd stepped it up for stopping by Sunny Farms.

Focus, Brightwood. In the middle of a heated discussion isn't the time to be ogling the man.

"My brother, Finn, rode along to pick up Honor today. Not some stranger, not some random guy. Who did you think would be with me?"

Ryker's upset visibly deflated. "I thought maybe a boyfriend. Wasn't sure."

"I'm not dating anyone. Wouldn't you know that by now?"

"I thought I did. I just—" His lips pressed together.

Had he been jealous? Could that explain part of the fiery reaction shooting from him over the last few minutes? A spark ignited in Charlie, blossoming at the thought.

"Growing up, my mom was the queen of bad boyfriends, and a couple of them, one in particular, really messed with me."

The baby ember was quickly snuffed out by trepidation. "Did he…" She was afraid to ask…and afraid to not ask and miss out on knowing more about this man in front of her. "Was he abusive?"

"Mostly verbal, though he shoved me around a time or two…" Ryker shrugged as if it didn't matter, but of course it did. "He still affects me every so often. Still sneaks into my mind, and I just… I have to protect Honor from something like that. When I saw your brother, it all came rushing back. Even his build—he's an imposing guy—reminded me of Bruce, who was my mom's boyfriend when I was in middle school. I guess the sight of him messed with me."

Middle school. So young. Not that there was ever a good age to suffer abuse. Tears pooled, and Charlie opened the grill under the guise of checking the burgers to hide her response from Ryker. He had his own emotions to deal with. He didn't need hers added on top.

"I'm sorry that happened to you. It shouldn't have. And I'm sorry that today triggered it. I can promise you my brother is the most kind and gentle man. Probably to a fault. I wouldn't let just anyone around Honor. She means too much to me."

Ryker's exhale shuddered. "Thank you."

Footsteps sounded on the wooden platform above them, but they were too light to be Finn's.

"Uncle Ry?" Honor peeked through the wooden slats and then scurried down the stairs. She barreled into Ryker, and he scooped her up, obviously struggling to send his painful past far away from the present.

Charlie began flipping burgers to give them a moment. Ryker had peeled back a layer of himself just now, and she was surprisingly grateful it had been with her.

When she'd walked down the stairs and spotted Ryker, she'd envisioned a repeat of the first night at the park. But after his revelation, his heightened response over seeing a man he didn't know with Honor made so much sense.

What didn't was the pinch of disappointment Charlie had felt when she'd realized his concerns were over Honor…and not jealousy over her.

Chapter Seven

"Were you fighting, Uncle Ry?" The tremor in Honor's question registered like a sledgehammer to the back of his knees.

How loud had their conversation been if Honor had come to that conclusion? He met Charlie's evergreen eyes over Honor's shoulder as he held on to the girl.

"No, Honor." Charlie must have read his panic, because her response was calm and confident. Reassuring. "We were just talking about some things."

Thank you. He silently mouthed the gratitude, and Charlie gave a slight nod, her cheeks creasing. She could easily have told Honor her uncle was a jerk, and it would have been true. He had shown up at Charlie's unannounced with a wasp under his collar.

When Charlie had come down her apartment stairs, Ryker had been sitting in his truck, trying to convince himself to leave and talk to her about his questions and concerns at the next visitation.

He'd failed, obviously.

"Mommy used to fight with CJ."

Ryker ran a hand over Honor's curls, and they sprang

back up like grass after a Texas rainstorm. "Did he ever hurt you?"

Honor's head shook. "I hidded in my room when he came over. He had mean eyes. Before he started coming over, Mommy was happy, but then she stopped playing princess with me 'cause she was tired."

Charlie's eyes shimmered. "I'm sorry, Honor. Even with all of that, I'm sure you miss your mom."

Her trembling lower lip agreed.

If only Ryker had a clue where Kaia had disappeared to. He'd left numerous messages on her dad's phone, but the man hadn't responded. And their mom didn't know anything regarding her daughter's whereabouts. During their last phone call, Mom had praised Ryker for moving to Colorado to take care of Honor and then gone on to explain why she couldn't do anything of the sort—because she was too old to be raising grandbabies.

In truth, she was simply focused on herself. She'd always had that tendency.

"Your mama might not be here right now—" Or ever again, for all he knew. " —but we are. And Charlie and I care about you so much. You're my favorite niece." She was his only niece, but the encouragement coaxed a smile around her ever-present fingernail.

"I got a part in the play at school."

"You did?" He and Charlie responded at the same time, and Ryker let Charlie continue.

"Which one?"

"Lily Lollipop."

His and Charlie's gazes collided, filled with curiosity, a look Ryker would imagine parents shared quite often. He'd have to unpack that thought later.

"Is that a good thing?" Charlie asked.

Her head bobbed. "Ms. Rana said I was too young for Carmony Candy so she gave me another part. It's got a yellow costume and it's so pretty and I'm so excited!"

The run-on earned relief and grins from her two adults.

"Good girl." Ryker hugged her again and then plunked her on the ground.

Charlie squeezed her next. "I'm so proud of you, Honor! You were so brave to try out." Her eyes crinkled when they met Ryker's. *Yeah, yeah, you were right*, they said. He chuckled at her unspoken admission.

"Charlie? Everything okay down there?" This time it was a woman's voice. Whoever was upstairs must be discussing them down here. Discussing their heated conversation, no doubt. Ryker wouldn't mind a rock to crawl under right about now.

"We're good," Charlie called up. "We just found out that Honor got a part in her school play."

"You did?" The woman pounded down the steps and joined them. "Good job, Honor girl." She held up her hand for a high five, and Honor participated with gusto. "Way to go." The woman's deep chocolate eyes turned on Ryker. She tucked back a lock of dark, straight hair while sizing him up. "And I hear you have a pretty good uncle to encourage you to try." His defenses eased. "I'm Addie. Charlie's closest and dearest friend whether she wants me to be or not."

"Ryker. And Charlie mentions you often, so I'd say your friendship is on equal footing."

Addie laughed. "It had better be." She bent to Honor's level, hands on her knees. "Do you know what this means, Honor?"

Her head shook.

"We have to turn dinner into a party. We have to celebrate you getting a part in the play!"

Based on the excitement and trepidation mingling across Honor's face, she didn't know what to think about that.

Addie must have also recognized Honor's concern because she continued. "Parties have to have dessert, right?"

Honor nodded solemnly, as if afraid she might get the answer wrong.

"Should we go inside and see what Sawyer's up to?" Addie held out her hand to the girl. "I'll show you what dessert I brought for later, and you can tell me more about this special part of yours."

They tromped up the stairs, leaving Ryker with Charlie once again. A smile ghosted her lips as she listened to their chatter fade.

He should really get out of here. He'd already interrupted enough of her night.

"Addie's the best to swoop in and celebrate Honor. I never had a girlfriend like her growing up. The kind to flip through *Seventeen* magazines with or paint nails."

Charlie happy and talking freely with him was mesmerizing. Maybe he could stay another minute. "Those are not things guys do."

"Me, either! It's just funny to not have had that as a kid when it felt like all the other girls did, and to find a friend like her as an adult..." She turned the grill and gas off. "It's a good thing, that's all I'm saying. I hope Honor finds a close friend for her growing-up years. Maybe it will be Gabby, maybe not. Who knows? But I pray there's another girl who's just right for her, because it's hard to be the odd girl out."

"Is that what you were?"

"Kind of. I guess. I'm not even sure. I was more… invisible."

"What do you mean by that?"

Charlie shook her head as if surprised she'd gone so far down the rabbit hole. "Nothing." She opened the grill and moved the burgers onto the clean plate she'd brought with her. The scent made his stomach let out a growl, thankfully too quiet to be caught. "We should head upstairs. Celebrate Honor."

We. Was that an invitation? And if yes, should he accept it? This was Charlie's world. She'd been overly gracious with him so far for butting into it. Yes, he wanted to celebrate Honor, but this wasn't his place. Was it? Or was it best for Honor if he and Charlie joined forces until he took over her care? They both knew that was where things were headed, right? Especially now that he had a job. Though it would be a few weeks until his first paycheck.

"How do you feel about staying to celebrate Honor? It's only Addie, her fiancé, Evan Hawke, my brother and then Addie's son, Sawyer. Not a huge crew."

"I—" He opened his mouth to discuss his concerns, and an agreement came out instead. "Sure. That would be great. She deserves some accolades…for surprising both of us."

"So, you did have doubts." Charlie handed him the dirty plate with the spatula on top and carried the one with the cooked burgers. He followed her as she headed for the stairs.

"Of course. Especially once you reamed me out. Then I was shaking in my boots that I was going to be wrong for letting her try and you'd hang me out to dry on the clothesline as punishment."

Charlie preceded him up the stairs, her chuckle quiet. "Not a bad idea. I'll have to file that away for future use." She stopped before opening the door, the two of them squished on the landing together. Charlie's fresh scent warred with the burgers, and Ryker refused to admit to himself which one triggered more interest at the moment. "In all seriousness, though, that makes me feel better that it wasn't just me struggling, wondering how things would turn out with this play. If she'd get hurt."

"You weren't alone, that's for sure." Perhaps it would be safer for both of them if Charlie *was* alone in all of this. But the minute Honor had forged a connection between them, that option had flown out the window.

Another thing Ryker had no intention of admitting? How thankful he was for that very thing.

Charlie's crew did a pretty impressive job of throwing together an impromptu party. Someone had found balloons in her junk drawer and blown them up. They'd added a "celebration candle" to Honor's piece of dessert. It had looked an awful lot like a birthday candle, but Honor hadn't cared. Charlie had never seen her so happy or excited. It was as if for one evening, the weight of the abandonment she constantly lived under had fallen away, leaving the raw and unfiltered version of the girl beneath visible.

"They are pretty stinking cute together." Addie's vision landed on Sawyer and Honor as she stood in the kitchen talking with Charlie. The kids were currently occupying one "room" of the tent/fort made of sheets the men had constructed in the living room. Ryker was camped out with them, attempting to play the memory game, though Sawyer kept messing up the cards. And Evan and Finn were seated at the breakfast bar, discussing the latest expedition Evan had led for trauma victims—a career that had sprouted because of his own experience enduring a below-the-knee amputation the summer before his senior year of high school. He'd recently relocated his trips to Colorado so that he could spend time with Addie and Sawyer in between the excursions.

"They are. Thank you for celebrating Honor like this. It was a good night. I think she needed it."

Addie's eyes, which were dark and gorgeous thanks to the Filipino heritage spilling down from her mom's side of the family, crinkled with amusement. "I think maybe you needed it, too."

"Definitely." Stress seeped out of her in one long exhale. "I can get so caught up in the details with Honor that I forget the big picture. A good day is a win. A good evening is a win. Sometimes just a good hour is a win."

"I'm the same way. The other day I was making a list of everything at the B & B that still needs an overhaul. I got so upset and overwhelmed that Evan made me stop and write a list of everything we've already done. It filled three pages. Sometimes we have to remember how far we've come, not just the goal of where we're going."

"I am terrible at that."

"You and me both, kid."

They discussed wedding plans and scrolled through bridesmaid dresses together, until eventually Addie announced that they had to get going. She'd kept her phone with her all night, but thankfully had only had to answer a few quick questions from B & B guests—one looking for an extra toothbrush and another inquiring about a steamer.

Evan rounded up a complaining Sawyer while Addie gathered her now-empty dessert dish. They exchanged hugs and goodbyes and made their way out the door.

Finn rounded the breakfast bar and hugged Charlie. "Guess I should head out, too. Thanks for dinner, sis."

"Anytime. I'm glad you'll be living here soon so that we can do this more often."

"Me, too." He said goodbye to Honor and Ryker, then opened the door and stepped outside onto the landing.

Charlie followed him, wrapping her cardigan tight around her as she did. The temperature had dropped since the sun slid behind the mountains.

"You okay?" Finn's quiet comment was meant for her ears only, and her head quirked.

"What do you mean?"

He pointed through the open door, to where Ryker remained with Honor. "He's not giving you any trouble? Things sounded pretty heated downstairs earlier."

Would the quietly playing Bluetooth speaker on her kitchen counter hide this conversation from Ryker?

Most likely.

"Overprotective much? I thought you liked him. You seemed to get along well tonight."

"We did. I do. I just…getting along with someone is different when my sister is involved. If you need anything, you'll let me know, right?"

"Of course." Not that she planned to require her brother's assistance. Charlie had marched into fostering with just her and God, and she trusted that her heavenly

Father had a plan in the messiness of what had become of Honor's situation. Although, it wasn't messy for both her and Ryker to be there for the girl. That only made sense. It was the jumbled emotions that came with the muddied waters that made it hard.

Finn left and Charlie went back inside, latching the door.

Ryker peeked out from under the sheet that blocked part of his body. "You okay if Honor and I finish this game?"

"Definitely." Charlie cleared dishes, catching pieces of their conversation. It wasn't eavesdropping if Ryker knew she could hear, right? She loaded items into the dishwasher—Evan had offered, sweet man, but Charlie had refused because she had a system as to what went where in the appliance. The dishes cleaned better and were easier to put away when they were organized. She mentally rolled her eyes at herself. Living alone for so long had turned her particular.

"Ah, you beat me," Ryker yelped, his upper body crashing to the floor as if Honor had taken a sword to his torso.

Charlie's eye roll was real and amused this time. The man had to quit letting Honor win at everything. But then, the girl probably needed the lift right now. Once her world settled again, they could impart more lessons about learning to lose well.

They. That was assuming she'd be around in the future. Highly unlikely if everything went according to plan. And Ryker getting a job today—especially one he was so excited about—was another step toward him taking over Honor's care.

Sadness exploded in Charlie, bigger and deeper than

she'd expected. She was definitely getting attached to Honor. Charlie had assumed this would happen, but she'd imagined the timeline to get to this point would take longer than it had.

"Honor, it's time to get ready for bed. And you need to take a shower tonight."

"But I don't want to. It's Friday and I don't have school tomorrow."

"A shower always feels good before bed. You'll be quick about it."

So far Honor had been anything but quick in her showers. Charlie wasn't sure what she did in there, but she would guess daydream was high on the list.

"But Uncle Ryker is here, and he never comes to play with me."

Actually, the man has seen you far more than the times he's been allotted, because of me, thank you very much.

Charlie opened her mouth to respond when she was cut off. "No arguing, Honor. You had a great party, and everyone was so excited about your part in the play. You'll ruin all of that if you throw a fit over a silly shower."

Well done. Charlie barely resisted clapping at Ryker's response.

Honor pushed up from the carpet as if her limbs were made of bricks. "Fine." Her little huff propelled her out of the fort and into the bathroom.

Ryker joined Charlie in the kitchen. "What do you want me to do first? Take down the fort or help with dishes?"

"You don't have to do either."

He didn't budge. "You sick of me? Need me out of

your hair?" When his vision followed his words, landing on her likely messy red locks, the faintest curve claimed his lips. It was subdued and attractive and distracting. "I like yours, by the way. I've never been a short-hair guy, but then you came along and blew that theory out of the water."

Oh. Her pulse cranked far too quickly for such an offhand comment. "Thanks?"

"You don't have to say it like a question."

She laughed. "Habit, I guess." Plus, receiving compliments was new for her. Especially from a guy like Ryker. Most of the time Charlie had been ignored by men. They just…didn't notice her. That's what she'd been about to get into downstairs when she'd been grilling. She'd always felt invisible. It wasn't just that guys weren't interested in her—it was as if they didn't even know she existed.

When she'd assumed the guy who'd been her friend in high school had liked her as much as she'd liked him, she'd not only found out otherwise, but quickly realized that he didn't consider their friendship to be as close as she did.

Charlie was wallpaper. Men didn't notice her until it was time to take the stuff down. Then she became a nuisance. She'd gotten used to it, so Ryker *seeing* her was…unusual. She wouldn't define it as bad. Only that she had to be careful not to read into his comments or attention.

Honor broke into song in the shower, her voice off-key and dramatically adorable.

"Does she do that often?"

"Not before tonight."

"Huh. Well, I guess that would make the evening a success, wouldn't it?"

"It was for me." Charlie returned to rinsing dishes in the sink.

"Me, too." Ryker was too close for comfort, holding out a hand for the dish she'd just finished rinsing. Charlie's fingers stuck to it before releasing. She could always redo the dishwasher later if Ryker loaded it haphazardly. "Thanks for letting me stay. It was over and above. I recognize that, in case you think I don't."

Well. That was nice of him.

"At first I thought it was going to be awkward staying after our conversation downstairs. Figured everyone knew we'd been—" he made air quotes "—'discussing' something." Ryker reached for the bowl in her sudsy hand. "And then I heard your brother checking on you like I'm a monster. And since I started out acting that way at the park the first night…ouch. That truth stung."

"You heard us over the music?"

"Bits and pieces."

Charlie scavenged for silverware beneath the bubbles and grabbed a handful. She brushed in front of Ryker to load them into the dishwasher, her skin buzzing at the fleeting contact. "It wasn't a terrible conversation downstairs. You had a moment where you almost lost it, but you pulled yourself together. No park Ryker made an appearance. And the reason behind your upset validated the inquisition."

He gave a slow nod, holding her captive with his soulful, sea-colored eyes. "And you reined me in. I needed it. You seem to have a calming effect on me."

Charlie's cheeks warmed. "I don't know about that."

"Thanks for listening and not engaging. Not fighting.

I'm sure I could have easily entered a shouting match for no reason beyond being triggered."

"You're welcome."

"And I'm sorry you had to do that for me at all."

Strangely enough, Charlie wasn't.

Charlie's close proximity was wreaking havoc on Ryker. When she'd moved in front of him to load the silverware, she hadn't retreated. What had they been talking about again? His gaze fell to her rose-colored lips. The temptation to kiss this woman who calmed him—who let him into her life and Honor's when she could have refused to do anything of the sort—was incredibly strong.

And those reasons he'd just listed were also why he had to keep things platonic. Stirring the pot with Charlie would affect things with Honor. The two of them weren't in a bubble. Ryker couldn't just throw caution to the side and follow any momentary feeling. Not like his mom would do.

He could consider Charlie cute when she scrunched her nose or when she tensed because he'd begun loading the dishwasher instead of her, but his focus right now was on his niece, and he refused to do anything to jeopardize gaining the right to care for her.

No matter how attractive and distracting he found Charlie.

The bathroom door banged open. Honor was dressed in her pajamas, wet hair dripping. "I'm going to be in a play. And I'm going to go on stage and say lots and lots of lines." Honor's feet thumped as she ran from the bathroom to her bedroom, that door also slamming like an exclamation point.

Charlie's face clicked into full-panic mode. "She has to memorize lines. Lots and lots of lines." She reached into the sink and absentmindedly retrieved a platter, which immediately began to slip through her wet, soapy fingers.

Ryker snagged it before it crashed. He added it to the row in the dishwasher Charlie had already started, wondering what all she'd rearrange after he left.

"Honor will be fine. She can do it. She's obviously excited about it, so that will help. And we have time, right? When is the play?"

"I think it's only like a month away, because they also do a Christmas one, so they need time to prepare for that."

That was fast. Ryker wrangled his doubts into submission so that Charlie wouldn't decipher them and continue down freak-out lane.

"We'll figure it out. You don't have to handle it alone. Unless…you want to." He just kept inserting himself without permission, didn't he? One of these times, Charlie would tell him she didn't need his help. That she was perfectly capable of caring for Honor on her own. And all of that would be true. She was the more successful of the two of them. Ryker was just a simple country boy who loved horses and the harmony they created in people's lives. He'd gotten his dream job today, and that was the thing—it was enough for him. He didn't need to own a business like Charlie. Didn't require a fat bank account. He just wanted an uncomplicated life.

It was likely Charlie regarded him with a hint of pity. She hadn't given that impression—or displayed it with her ever-changing facial expressions—but Ryker wouldn't be surprised if she thought it.

The Bruce-isms that had driven his worthlessness deep inside him as a kid lived on with a vengeance that surprised Ryker, and sometimes he still believed them. Believed that his contentment, his lack of desire to do more than work with horses or help teens in the way he'd been helped…that it somehow made him less than. In the morning, under bright lights, he could see untruth in those convictions. But in the dark, the lies grew real and concrete like monsters under the bed.

"I'll take the help. Memorizing always came easy to me, so if it doesn't for Honor, I don't have a clue how to help her."

"Have no fear. When it comes to cramming for tests, I'm your man."

Charlie's pupils widened, and Ryker winced internally. This was what he got for trying to be charming and funny and encouraging. He shot himself in the foot with a wannabe statement that could never come to fruition.

Chapter Eight

At four o'clock on Tuesday, Charlie said goodbye to Scott, left her coveralls on the hook in the office, cleaned up and escaped out the front door of the shop.

She was on her way to check on the construction next door when her name being called stopped her, and she turned.

Her brother jogged to catch up. "What are you up to?"

"Checking out progress at the café. Want to walk through with me?"

"Sure." He opened the door for her, and the two of them stepped inside. The space was long and lean. Charlie envisioned a countertop along the right, with cabinets behind for storage and supplies. People would order there, and then they could sit wherever and hang out as long as they liked.

The place would require a ton in terms of setup, but that would be a long stretch down the road—once the construction was closer to completion, not in the infancy stages. And then she'd have to put out feelers for a manager. Someone who could handle a simple menu and supplies and hiring. Charlie would be involved, of course, but she couldn't manage both places on her own, so she'd need to hire someone qualified and trustworthy to step in.

Finn inspected this and that, acting like he knew anything about construction. He didn't. He was much more versed in ranching—he'd worked at one during and after high school and then had spent a couple of years working the guest ranch scene at Wilder Ranch before deciding he wanted to be his own boss. He'd dedicated a few years to working oil rigs in order to save up the cash to make the purchase of a ranch possible. Charlie was proud of him *and* glad he was alive, because rigging could be dangerous. During Finn's first year, a young coworker had died his first day on the job due to an explosion. Working as a drill floor hand kept Finn busy and exhausted. Charlie was more than ecstatic that such a hazardous phase would finally be coming to an end.

Finn had wandered down the hallway that led to the back exit and now returned to her. "I'm heading back to North Dakota. Going to give notice and pack my things. I'm closing mid-October on the ranch."

"That's great news." Wasn't it? "Are you moping because you're going to miss me while you're gone?" Charlie waited for his trademark grin, but it didn't surface. "Why do you look like your dog just died?" Finn scrubbed a hand across his chin. Was he buying time or searching for words? "Whatever it is, just say it. I'm a big girl. I can handle it." What was it with the men surrounding her lately not spitting things out? First Ryker and now Finn.

"I think you should be careful with Ryker." The admission tumbled out quickly, like water over slippery rocks in a mountain stream. "It's messy with you fostering Honor and him being involved. I would assume that's unusual."

"Our situation might not be the norm, but once Angela asked me to supervise, things just sort of snowballed. It's not like we can hide from each other in a town this size." And Charlie had been praying so consistently about all of it that she felt confident that letting Ryker have access to Honor was the right thing to do. Angela had confirmed as much, saying that Ryker had already completed the courses she'd required of him. If he was able to follow through on the rest, the girl would be moved to kinship care with her uncle.

Charlie had accepted that. For the most part. Sure, there was still a smidgen of her that held out on trusting him completely. She couldn't keep that sliver of niggling concern from bobbing to the surface once in a while. Probably exactly what Finn felt.

"I'm not denying that Ryker's a nice guy. I'm impressed with what he's willing to do and give up for Honor. To take care of her. I respect that. But I don't see why you have to be so involved in all of this. Just seems like you're going to get hurt. Either by something he does or by losing the girl."

Charlie grabbed a broom and began sweeping up construction debris, relocating it to the corner. The place wouldn't be put together for a while, but doing something, anything, made her feel better. "Hurt is part of existing. People make mistakes and mess things up. I get your concern. I do. But there's not much I can change about the situation. Ryker and I are connected now, whether we want to be or not. Honor is a tie between us."

Finn's concern registered in two lines that split his brow. "I get that. Just…be careful."

She forced a smile, but it was like lifting a slab of granite with her pinkie finger. "Always."

Shouldn't he be supporting her decisions like she had for him over the years? Why couldn't Finn trust her? And God? Charlie wasn't in this alone. She'd gone to the source many, many times regarding Ryker. The last thing she needed right now was doubt. Something Finn had just buried her under like Honor dumping sand with her new truck.

They said goodbye and parted ways, and Charlie left to meet Ryker, of all people, to work on painting the set for the play.

While she'd appreciated his previous offer to cover their volunteer shift, she still wanted to be involved. Plus, now that he was working at Sunny Farms—had started yesterday—his time was limited, too. They'd agreed to take an evening shift tonight, and Addie had picked Honor up after school and kept her for a play-date with Sawyer. The two of them had a three-year age gap, but they'd enjoyed playing with each other on Friday. Addie had already texted to say that Honor was so entertaining for Sawyer that she'd crossed a bunch of items off her to-do list.

When Charlie arrived at the school, Ryker was already there. She wore ancient, torn-at-the-knees jeans and an equally vintage T-shirt. Ryker had also donned older jeans, a simple white T-shirt, plus tennis shoes and a baseball cap. Her stomach squeezed. *Just noticing him isn't a crime.* A motto she repeated more often than she cared to admit.

Charlie wasn't sure if she was relieved or annoyed to see that she wasn't the only one who'd *noticed* Ryker. One of the moms—single, based on her left hand—was standing awfully close to him while painting. And unlike Charlie, she'd donned fashionable workout gear for the job. Charlie had never owned workout gear, and the last place she'd ever attempt to look cute was at a gym. Weren't workout clothes supposed to be for sweating and exercising? Or for lounging around at home while watching TV?

She found a spot two backdrops down from Ryker, asked for directions on what needed to be done and got to work while Finn's cautionary advice sat like an elephant on her conscience.

Her brother's concerns equaled an unsolvable mechanical issue, and Charlie didn't know how to heed his warning while still fostering Honor. Right now, if the girl was involved in her life, her uncle was, too. Charlie couldn't just jump backward in their relationship and switch to only seeing or talking to Ryker during visitations. It would raise too many suspicions from everyone, including Honor.

As if hearing her thoughts, the man showed up at her side, giving her arm a nudge with his because she didn't stop working to acknowledge him.

"Hey, I didn't know you were here. When did you show up?"

"Couple of minutes ago. You were busy." Charlie cringed. *Jealous much?* Ryker was completely off-limits because of Honor, and yet, her green side had reared its ugly head. Maybe Finn was right. She should run. "You were already painting," she clarified in a calm and hopefully nonsuspect voice. "So I found a spot that needed work and got to it." She could only pray that if Ryker were to detect her strange bout of jealousy, he'd ignore it, because that's exactly what she planned to do.

Thanks a lot, Finn. Before this, talking with Ryker had been easy. But her brother shining a spotlight on their relationship, forcing her to dissect it, had made things weird.

Just when she felt like she and Ryker had finally found steady footing, her brother had caused an earthquake.

Ryker switched brushes so that he could work on the forest backdrop with Charlie. She was acting strange, and his curiosity over why was spiking.

"Honor okay?"

Charlie nodded, concentrating on filling in a small cloud in the middle of blue sky. Someone had penciled in what needed to be painted and then left notes of what colors were to be used for each space. Foolproof.

"She's at Addie's, hanging out with Sawyer for a bit."

"Good." He moved from one green section to another small one. "They had fun together the other night."

Charlie leaned closer to the canvas to tackle an intricate swirl. "That doesn't bother you?"

"What part? That Honor wants to play with a toddler?"

The conversation to their right—including the cougar who'd been all over him when he'd arrived—grew boisterous, twisting Ryker's stomach. Not his style. He was only here for Honor, which he'd politely tried to explain. Though he wasn't sure Mrs. Robinson had listened—or that he could remember the woman's real name. The one from the book and movie fit so much better.

"No. That she's connecting to other people who aren't...you."

Strange question. "Why would I be upset that Honor

is connecting with other people? Good people? That's exactly what I want for her. What she should have had all along. That would be my prayer for her, actually, that she'd be surrounded by a community who knows and loves her, and nothing like what happened to her when my sister messed up ever happens again."

"Huh." The under-her-breath sound was accompanied by more painting, less talking from Charlie. She must be processing something. Or upset?

"You seem off today."

Her paintbrush momentarily paused. "Weird day, I guess."

She didn't elaborate, so Ryker continued to work. Charlie usually wasn't melodramatic. In fact, with everything that had been thrown at her, she'd been nothing but calm and sensible. Always putting Honor first—even when it meant putting up with him.

Maybe he was the issue. Maybe she'd reached her limit in dealing with him. Or maybe she'd just had a rough day.

He couldn't help wanting to erase some of what was eating at her.

Before he thought it through, his paintbrush jabbed out and grazed her cheek.

She jumped. "What was that for?"

"Accident. Sorry." He stemmed a smile, and Charlie quirked her head as if trying to figure him out. After a second, she returned to her task. How could she believe him? He'd just painted her face. Did she really have no idea what he was up to?

Ryker reached over her to paint something above her head, crowding her on purpose. She shrank down a little but kept focused on painting. *Seriously, woman.*

He nudged her more obviously this time, and she gave a squeak of indignation as her brush jutted outside the lines.

"*Ack.* Now I'm going to have to fix that." She stepped back from the canvas, eyes narrowed in his direction. "What are you doing? Trying to get me fired from painting the set?"

He mustered every ounce of innocence he possessed. "I was just reaching that spot. Sorry."

Her suspicion lingered, had him fighting laughter. Ryker used the opportunity to return to the scene of the crime and add more paint to her cheek that he'd previously marred.

"You've got a little something right there." He added another swipe. "Oops. It's just getting bigger. Let me see if I can—"

Charlie leaped back from him. "Ryker whatever-your-middle-name-is Hayes, that is enough!"

"It's Damon." And the thought of Charlie using it was way too intriguing to him. The fact that she was off-limits wasn't even on his radar right now.

Charlie snagged a small yellow paintbrush and wrote *a-n-n-o-y-i-n-g* across the chest of his white three-to-a-package T-shirt. He laughed. At least he'd finally gotten through to her.

Her mouth arched, registering like a throat punch, and when she laughed, everything was right in the world again. "What has gotten into you?"

"This is how painting is supposed to go. Didn't you know that?"

"I must have missed that instruction while growing up." Her eyes danced, sparkling and playful. To think that he'd had anything to do with her change of demeanor was intoxicating stuff.

Charlie sent her brush up and down the inside of his arm, covering his tattoo in yellow paint.

"You do realize the only reason I'm not retaliating with a bucket of paint right now is because we're in public."

"Maybe." Charlie's teeth pressed into her bottom lip, then gave way to amusement that sent his pulse skittering teenage-crush fast.

"So then you also understand that I'm going to have to get you back for this at some point." His nod encompassed the tattoo.

"No. This makes us even. And now I think we can just forget this ever happened."

"I don't." And how wrong was he to look forward to whatever moment brought him back into close proximity with Charlie? Close enough to touch her, to inhale that sweet lemon scent.

Her thumb slid along the writing on his forearm, clearing away paint like a windshield wiper.

"What does it mean?" Ryker had gotten the tattoo in Hebrew because he hadn't wanted people to be able to read his innermost thoughts. He must have paused too long, because she continued. "You don't have to tell me if you don't want to. I'm being nosy."

She wasn't. More likely Charlie just wanted to know him better. Especially since he'd wormed his way into her life in order to be near Honor.

"It means 'worthy' in Hebrew."

Those forest green eyes of hers melted. "He doesn't own you." Her voice had that steel edge he'd come to expect from her. Not mean. Hardly ever that. Just strong.

Attractive. "He was a weak man who preyed on a kid in order to make himself feel strong. Nothing he said to you is true. You're caring and kind and safe…and definitely worthy. That man does *not* define you."

Those words were extra sweet coming from the woman he'd frightened when he'd first barreled into town.

"He doesn't. I know who does, but sometimes I just need the reminder." He shrugged to make light of something that was anything but.

"We all do." Charlie squeezed his arm before letting go. She cleaned her hands on a rag and went back to painting, a smile playing on her lips, leaving Ryker feeling like he deserved his tattoo for once, because he was the one who'd helped put it there.

After her volunteer shift working on the set, Charlie drove to Addie's to pick up Honor. Addie welcomed her into the kitchen, where she was prepping breakfast for the next day.

"How'd it go over here?"

"They were great together. Having Honor around to entertain Sawyer was such a help that I feel like I should pay her for babysitting. They're building something out of Duplos right now on the dining room table."

"That's a relief. I knew Honor would love to play with Sawyer. I just hoped she wouldn't make things harder for you."

"Are you kidding? It was easier to have two than one. They kept each other occupied. Honor played teacher, and Sawyer was supposed to be her pupil. Though he didn't sit still or learn anything as far as I could tell." Addie grabbed a mug from the cupboard. "You have time for a hot chocolate? The kids already had theirs, because of course I had to reward their good behavior with sugar. As any good honorary foster auntie would do."

"I do have time. And I was also a good girl today."

"Then hot chocolate you shall have." Addie doctored the drink with cocoa and milk and fresh whipped cream, then handed it over to Charlie.

Charlie palmed the warm mug. "Thanks."

"So, how was painting?" Addie leaned against the counter facing Charlie.

"Confusing." She took a careful sip of the hot, delicious liquid.

Addie nodded solemnly, though her eyes twinkled. "Painting is usually that."

"Ha. It was just, before I went, Finn had this conversation with me about Ryker. He thinks I should be careful with him, not let him in too much. But we're basically in this together at this point. Unless he doesn't follow through on what Angela has asked of him, and I do think he will."

"I do, too. He seems to really love Honor."

"I agree. When I first met him, I wouldn't have said that. Obviously. But now I can see who he really is."

"I get where Finn is coming from, but you're the most levelheaded person I know. You'll handle this. You and God. He's the one who laid it on your heart to foster in the first place. He'll see you through."

It was nice to hear Addie embracing her faith. God had been a new concept for her not too long ago.

"I had time to process on the way here, and I realized that Finn is allowed to have concerns. So am I, for that matter. But that doesn't mean I'm going to stop living or stop having any connection with Ryker."

"That makes sense. It's one of those situations that's really out of your control."

"Yep." Charlie felt that unknown future down to the marrow of her bones.

"Was the painting also confusing because you thought you were supposed to include your face in the festivities?"

Charlie's hand crept up to her cheek. "I thought I'd gotten all that off."

Addie beamed as if she was privy to what had made the spot appear in the first place. "Did you walk into the canvas or…"

"Ryker was being a goof."

"Oh, he was, was he? By the way, before I met Ryker, you never mentioned that it's not exactly a chore to look at the man."

Charlie swirled her hot chocolate, finding the liquid *quite* mesmerizing. "Guess I hadn't noticed."

Addie snorted. "And now I find out he was flirting with you while painting."

"He wasn't flirting!"

"Then how did the paint end up on your cheek?"

"I was in kind of a mood when I got there because of Finn's admonition." Charlie kept out the part about arriving to find the other mom attached to Ryker like a fly on picnic food. That would only fuel Addie's current line of questioning. "Ryker must have known or sensed it, because he kept poking at me."

"And what was your response to that?"

"I poked back. It worked. He got me out of my head."

"Flirting will do that to you."

"It wasn't—" She was protesting an awful lot. *Had* Ryker been flirting with her? She didn't know, because she was awful at it. Didn't really understand how it worked. The girls in high school had flipped their hair and giggled when a boy said something that wasn't even funny, but there had to be more to it than that. Maybe she should have taken a class on the art of flirting instead of burying her head in engines. "At least I don't think it was."

"Okay." Addie's grin was very much like a pup who'd come across a plate of people food.

"It wouldn't make any sense for Ryker to be flirting with me. We're both in this for Honor. It's not about us. It's about her."

"Okay."

Addie's repeated acquiescence wasn't helping anything. Not when it came with a side of sass and amusement. Sure, feelings for Ryker were knocking at the back door, trying to distract Charlie. But it wouldn't be prudent to engage or even entertain the idea of something happening between them. Not with so much regarding Honor still up in the air. Plus, Charlie didn't get the impression that Ryker had any romantic inclinations toward her. Sure, she tended to be naive when it came to men, but he'd been nothing but platonic. Even today, if that had been flirting, it had barely been flirting.

Ryker Damon Hayes didn't feel anything for Charlie beyond the fact that she was currently his niece's caregiver. And just because Addie thought differently didn't make it true.

Chapter Nine

After work on Wednesday, Ryker called Kaia's dad for the umpteenth time while he drove back to town. Why didn't the man ever call or text back? If he didn't answer this time, Ryker would find a way to force the issue.

As if somehow sensing his threat, a gruff voice full of annoyance answered.

"Mr. Delaney." *Finally.* "It's Ryker Hayes." He cut right to the chase. "I really need to know if Kaia is okay. Have you heard from her?"

"I don't know anything." The man's reply was too quick, too curt. Something was up or off.

"Well, I'm at the point where I'm wondering if I need to call the police and report her as missing. I get that she might have needed to blow off steam after losing custody of Honor, but she's been gone for over two weeks now, and there's still no sign of her. I'm worried. So unless you can tell me something—that at least she's okay—I guess that's what I'll have to do."

Silence reigned for at least thirty seconds, and Ryker let it. He couldn't shake the sense that the man knew *something* about his daughter. Otherwise, wouldn't he be stressing regarding her whereabouts?

"She's fine."

That was all Milton Delaney offered, but Ryker latched on, relief cascading through him. *Thank You, God.*

He gripped the phone tighter in his hand. "Can you give me anything else? Does she need anything? Is she doing okay? Tell her that Honor—"

"I have nothing else to say." Kaia's dad hung up.

Ryker sighed and tossed the phone onto the seat of his truck. At least he could stop worrying that something had happened to Kaia, though now his curiosity was through the roof. Just what was his sister up to?

He parked outside the house where he'd rented a room. Even with the landlords requiring a full month's payment, he was still saving money over the Lazy Bones Motel, though of course he missed those luxurious accommodations desperately.

Despite currently being a sieve for expenses, Ryker was doing everything as affordably as he could. He'd had a small savings account in Texas, which was the only thing still keeping him afloat. He just wasn't sure how much longer it would last. Between now and his first Sunny Farms paycheck, he needed to make the smallest dent possible in his dwindling reserves.

After showering and changing into jeans and a T-shirt, Ryker threw together some bread, turkey and mayo and hopped back in his truck. He was supposed to be helping Honor with her lines for the play tonight, but working late at Sunny Farms—something he couldn't afford *not* to do—had him running behind. He'd texted Charlie to let her know, but she hadn't responded.

Guess communicating with him was on everyone's back burner.

Ryker wolfed down the pathetic excuse for a sandwich on the way over. When he parked and got out of his truck, he wiped crumbs from his shirt and jeans before heading up the wooden stairs to Charlie's well-lit apartment.

He gave a quick knock. "It's me."

The door swung open, and Charlie barely spared him a glance as she waved him inside. She wore ripped jeans with a fitted T-shirt that looked soft and worn and showcased a logo so faded he couldn't decipher it.

Ryker shut the door behind him. Honor was at the breakfast bar, numerous stacks of papers in front of her, and the tension in the room was Jell-O thick and just as wobbly.

"How are the lines going?"

Charlie raked a hand through her short red locks. "We haven't gotten to them yet. We've been working on some school stuff."

Honor perked up, her body straightening from slouched to interested. "But now that Uncle Ry is here, we're going to memorize lines for the play, right?"

"I don't know," Charlie chimed in. "We still have plenty to do."

"I don't want to do any of this stuff." Honor shoved the stack of papers and then hopped down from her stool. She stalked off to her bedroom, slamming the door with more force than her little frame should be able to muster.

Huh. Interesting. "So…how's it going over here?" For the first time since Ryker had met her, tears pooled in Charlie's eyes.

"Honor's school called today. She's way behind." Charlie plopped onto one of the stools that lined the breakfast bar and dropped her forehead into her palm.

"Behind on what?" Ryker rounded the bar and scanned the papers. Some had math, some letters. Others looked like they had something to do with reading.

"Pretty much everything." Charlie straightened papers, separating the ones Honor had completed from the blanks. "The teacher sent me some packets of things Honor needs to work on at home in order to catch up."

"And you've been working on this stuff since after school?"

Charlie glanced at the clock on the microwave. "We stopped for dinner."

Wow. That was a *lot* of extra work. No wonder Honor had thrown a hissy fit. Ryker sat on the third stool, leaving one between them so that he could face Charlie.

"With what she's been through, I'm not surprised she's behind. Are you?"

Charlie rubbed fingertips under her lower lashes. "I don't know. I guess not." She toyed with the edge of the papers. "She's so smart. It's just hard to think that's not coming through at school."

"She's definitely smart." Ryker motioned to the printed sheets. "None of this changes that. But I'm sure Kaia wasn't working with her before kindergarten. Add to that the fact that she was ripped from her mom, or her mom from her... I guess I'm not shocked by this development."

"True." Charlie squared her shoulders. "It's my job to help her, but she's been ornery about it from the moment we started working on this stuff tonight. How is she ever going to improve if she refuses to try?"

Sweet, strong, overachieving Charlie. Not everyone could rule the world with such precision. Especially not a hurting five-year-old.

He scooted down a stool so that they were next to each other and kept his voice low. "I doubt that she's completely unwilling to try. She's probably just tired from a long day at school. Remember when we went to kindergarten? We had half days. It's a lot for her. Especially since she only turned five in June. Maybe her age has something to do with all of this. Who knows? But emotionally, she might need to ride the slow train right now. I think a lot of this will work itself out once she feels settled and safe." He held up a finger. "And I'm not saying you're not providing that environment for her. Just that she's been through a lot in the last couple of weeks."

Charlie swallowed, her gaze cast downward. "I thought if we got right on it she'd improve quickly and not fall even more behind. That she'd fit in."

"Is that really what this is about? Fitting in?"

Those mesmerizing eyes of hers turned sorrowful. "No. I just want her to succeed. If I can help her—"

"You *are* helping her. You're amazing." He covered her hand with his. "You could direct a million-dollar company with only half of your attention span." That earned a faint lifting of her lips. "Do I think Honor can turn this stuff around with school? Yes. Probably. With time. It took her a while to get where she's at. It's going to take a bit to get her out of it." He tempered his next comment with a grin. "And I don't think you can reverse all of it in one night."

Charlie half laughed, half groaned. "That's what I

was doing, wasn't it? Did God lure me into fostering so that He could show me how inept I am at life?"

Ryker chuckled. "Actually, you're about the most equipped person I know. Which is probably why this is hard for you. Wanting to fix this and help Honor isn't a bad thing. It's who you are. But you're going to have to slow down to a more normal human pace this time because it involves someone outside of yourself." Her features turned begrudgingly amused. Good. Ryker was glad he hadn't offended her. "And no, I don't think that's how He works."

"Should we still let her do the play? She has so much to catch up on."

We. Finally that word was coming from Charlie's direction, too, and not just from him. "Maybe it's not a bad idea to let her keep doing the play because she's so excited about it. It's probably good for her to have something she's looking forward to. Plus, she'll be with other kids, making friends, learning something new. She's even going to figure out how to memorize and say lines in front of an audience."

"Lines." Panic sprouted wrinkles across Charlie's forehead. "I spent so much time on the school stuff tonight that we haven't even started on them."

"She'll be fine. We'll knock them out." Providing that memorizing wasn't incredibly hard for Honor. Not a concern Ryker planned to bring up as a possibility right now.

"Okay." Charlie inhaled and released two deep breaths. "So, I talked you down from freaking out after you saw Finn in my car, and now you've done the same for me over Honor being behind…in kindergarten."

His mouth curved to match hers. "We make a good

team." Surprising. Especially with how they'd started out. "On my way here, I saw that the nursery down the street has pumpkins out front. Maybe we should walk down there with Honor and get some for carving. Take a break. Sounds like she's done plenty tonight in terms of work."

"Because of her taskmaster."

"Because of her superhero foster mom."

Mom. That word had just dropped from his tongue. Charlie could never replace Kaia, but she'd done so much for Honor already, in such a short amount of time. She loved the girl sacrificially, that was for sure.

It made Ryker question why someone like Kaia, who struggled to make good decisions, would end up with a child, when someone like Charlie—who was so put together and safe and loving—didn't have the family she was obviously made for.

"That sounds like a really good idea. Do you want to mention it to her?"

"I think you should."

The corners of Charlie's eyes crinkled as if she knew exactly what he was doing. Letting her suggest the outing to Honor would ease the turmoil that had been simmering between them when he'd walked through the door.

When Charlie called for Honor, she came out of her room slowly, her pout in full effect. Once Charlie explained their offer—giving both of them credit—the hurt cleared from Honor's expression.

"I want to do that."

"Then let's go." Charlie popped up from her stool and retrieved a sweater from the coat closet. "Grab your jacket, Honor. It's supposed to cool down overnight."

The girl practically flew to her room.

Ryker pushed off from his stool. "I'll grab another layer from my truck when we go down. I was thinking we could carve the pumpkin later since we won't have time tonight—like maybe on Sunday after church? That way we can use the activity as a prize of sorts once Honor has finished out this week and done her extra work each day."

"Smart. I like it. Sunday works for me, and I think there will be a lot less fighting that way." Charlie's lips bowed. "And I'll be sure to keep things to fifteen or twenty minutes a day. Nothing crazy."

"Good. We can come up with some more prizes, too. I always needed some external motivation to care about school."

"Oh yeah? And what was that?"

"Usually it had something to do with a girl. Like in sixth grade when I realized how smart Michelle Star was and thought getting better grades might make her want to be my girlfriend." Michelle had never signed up to be his girlfriend, but Ryker had gotten better marks that quarter. "You women hold a lot of power."

"Maybe some do, but I've never been that type."

You are now. Yes, Ryker cared about Honor's schoolwork, but he also assumed she would figure things out in her own time, at her own pace. Likely when her emotions weren't so bruised and raw. But a big draw to why he felt the need to step in was to make things easier for Charlie. To make sure she was okay and not stressing.

So while Charlie might not think she was the type to influence a guy's actions...on this account, she'd be wrong.

* * *

Charlie had assumed picking out a pumpkin would be a short-lived activity. She'd assumed incorrectly. Honor had spent as much time inspecting, holding and analyzing pumpkins as most women would allot for choosing a wedding dress.

She was currently distracted by the gourd section. "It's so cute." Her whisper, directed at the small green one she held, was filled with far too much longing for a garden vegetable not grown for consumption.

"Why don't you pick out a few gourds plus a pumpkin? We can put the gourds out for fall decoration."

Honor's eyes grew wide at Charlie's offer. "Okay."

Charlie sidled up to Ryker, keeping her voice low enough that Honor wouldn't overhear. "Do you think she's never picked out a pumpkin before?"

His shrug and the concerned pucker claiming his brow said he'd been asking himself the same question.

Honor examined each gourd as if she was choosing a puppy instead of a perishable decoration. At this rate they would be here all night. But getting to see the joy on her face over such a small thing was definitely worth it. Ryker had been right—this was way more fun than schoolwork. And he'd also been right that tutoring Honor in small chunks of time made a lot more sense. As opposed to jumping into the deep end and forcing Honor to swim until exhaustion pulled her under—like Charlie had done when she'd heard from Honor's teacher and immediately determined to fix all the things.

She thanked God that Honor's uncle had barreled into their lives when he had. What would Charlie have done without him during these last two weeks? It was crazy to think that it had only been half a month since their lives had crashed into one another's. With all the time they'd spent together, Charlie felt as if she'd known Ryker much longer.

"I like this one." Honor handed the white gourd to Charlie. "And this one." The next had green and yellow stripes.

"What about this little guy?" Ryker held up a gourd that resembled a miniature pumpkin.

"I already pickeded two." Stress bogged down Honor's whisper.

Oh, sweet girl. You can have a million gourds if it helps you understand that you're loved and noticed and not alone.

"I think you should choose a third so that we can put them in a bowl. And two wouldn't be enough."

Honor nodded. After copious amounts of deliberation—and some prompting from Ryker—she chose a third. The same one Ryker had previously suggested.

Charlie met Ryker's matching smile as the girl skipped outside to deliberate over pumpkins. Cooler air met them when they followed, the breeze picking up speed as it rustled the leaves still clinging to branches.

The small shop sold some local vegetables along with plants and small trees. Charlie had never visited before, but the quaint place made her want to return. Though next year at this time she likely wouldn't have need of a pumpkin. She highly doubted she'd do any carving without Honor to instigate.

Unless I foster again. An ache grew and expanded at that. There was still too much up in the air for her to know what the future held. Charlie much preferred to have a game plan, but fostering was all about reacting to each moment.

Pumpkins were spread across the ground, and some were perched on a vintage trailer. The wooden base was worn and warped, but the setup would make for a cute photo.

"Honor, will you sit up there with the pumpkins? I want to take a picture."

The girl contemplated seriously before finally agreeing.

Ryker picked her up and set her on the edge of the trailer. Surrounded by a sea of orange and wearing her pink belted jacket—an impulse buy that Charlie hadn't been able to resist—Honor could model for the place's brochure.

After snapping a few, Charlie held out her palm to Ryker. "Give me your phone. Let me get one for you."

He complied with less grumbling, clearing a spot to sit next to Honor. Charlie took a couple of shots, her breaths shortened by the sting expanding inside her rib cage.

If only these two were her people. If only she didn't have to start over with hoping and praying for a family of her own once fostering Honor was done.

"Let's take one with the three of us." Ryker's suggestion interrupted her mopefest. Charlie joined them, and Ryker held up his phone and snapped a few selfies.

Honor went back to combing through pumpkins after their impromptu photo shoot, dismissing any that had black marks or strange spots or flat areas.

"I should have offered to take one of the two of you." Ryker winced. "I totally missed that, sorry."

"It's okay. We've taken some photos together." Enough that Charlie wouldn't have to wonder if the memory of Honor was real or not. She had the proof on her phone…and etched into a place on her heart that would always relish getting to love Honor. "She is serious about her pumpkin picking." Charlie copped a seat on the trailer as they watched her, and Ryker did the same next to her.

The place was quiet tonight, maybe because it was a school night or perhaps because it was still early in the season. Most people probably didn't pick out their pumpkins until mid-October.

"She is. What you asked me earlier—about if Honor had ever picked out a pumpkin before—the answer is, I'm not sure. Which made me angry at my sister all over again. I know she was a good mom because I witnessed it. Not perfect, by any means, but none of us are that. I know she loved Honor. Loves Honor."

"Do you think the boyfriend had anything to do with sending her so off course?"

"I think he had everything to do with it. That's around the time I stopped hearing from Kaia. And when her neighbor said she noticed changes, too. Kaia lost her job…it must have all been a spiral." Ryker's exhale held the weight of regret. "I finally talked to her dad today, and it was a good thing he answered, because I was about to lose my mind. He admitted she's okay. Or fine. And that was it. He wouldn't give me any more details."

"How frustrating. I'm sorry." Charlie picked up a yellow leaf and twirled it. "At least you know she's alive and okay in some way, shape or form."

"Exactly. Seems like he's covering for her. Trying to protect her somehow. She was charged with neglect but not arrested, which I guess happens. Maybe she's afraid of returning to Westbend? If I could talk to her, then I could figure out what's going through her head and help her."

"You're a good brother, Ryker."

He snorted. "If I was a good brother, I would've caught wind of her derailing earlier and stepped in to help."

"I get that. I do. We can all play the blame game on repeat. But ultimately, Honor isn't yours, and it wasn't your job to raise her."

"I know. But it still stinks."

"It does." While Charlie wanted to encourage Ryker, she also understood his position, because if she were in his boots, she'd likely fight the same guilt and follow the same path he had. It said a lot about him that he cared so much—about his sister and Honor.

Charlie tucked her hands into her sweater pockets as the wind kicked up a few notches. The predicted cold front was heading their way.

"Whoa." Ryker burrowed deeper into his lined flannel. "Weather's turning. We should probably pack up. Head back."

"Your Texas is showing, Hayes."

"So." He leaned closer, the faint scent of his soap tempting her senses. "You're telling me you're not ready to get out of here?"

His playful smile and close proximity were torturous, sending her stomach spiraling to her toes and the temperature skyrocketing. Charlie was about to fan herself when a new gust whipped past them, turning her bones to ice.

She whooped. "I'm definitely ready. Honor, pick a pumpkin before we all turn into Popsicles!"

Ryker hopped down from the trailer, then turned and

held out a hand to assist her. "I think your Colorado is broken, Brightwood."

His fingers were somehow warm and right at home against hers. *I think my heart is a little off-kilter, too.*

After some encouragement, Honor chose a pumpkin. They were about to check out when she panicked.

"Aren't you guys getting pumpkins, too?"

They hadn't been planning on it.

"We all need to carve them together."

"Of course we're getting pumpkins," Charlie filled in. "We just forgot. Silly us."

Charlie and Ryker made quick work of grabbing pumpkins and paying, and they started the walk back home.

"Are we going to carve these tonight?" Honor asked.

"We don't have time tonight," Ryker answered. "But I was thinking that if you do your extra schoolwork without complaining the rest of this week, we can carve them on Sunday afternoon."

Honor contemplated that for the next few steps. "Okay. I guess."

Charlie and Ryker's grins met over her head at her lackadaisical response. "We'll work on the extra school stuff a little each day. We won't do nearly as much as we did tonight, okay?"

"All right." More agreement laced her tone this time.

When a blast of cold skirted around them, they all picked up the pace. At Charlie's apartment, Ryker suggested that he and Honor check out her lines for the play.

Charlie prepped her lunch for tomorrow and packed Honor's as the two of them sat at the breakfast bar together.

"First line is 'I want to play in the fairy forest.'" He

shot Charlie an amused look, then repeated the line, adding rhythm to the words. When he broke into a terrible rap, Honor playfully screeched and covered her ears. But in seconds she'd abandoned her dramatics and joined in.

By the time Charlie finished lunches and prepping items for dinner tomorrow night, they'd done three lines like that—silly, with rhythm, memorable.

Ryker didn't make the experience last nearly as long as Charlie had with the extra schoolwork. Jerk.

When they finished, Charlie asked Honor to shower. She ran off without having to be told twice. Through the bathroom door, they heard her repeating her lines in the same goofy manner.

"Show-off." Charlie tossed the cheeky comment Ryker's way before opening the fridge and grabbing a sparkling water. "You want anything?"

"No, thanks. I'm pretty exhausted. I think I'm going to take off if that's cool."

"Of course. No problem." She prayed Ryker couldn't decipher her disappointment. For some reason she'd expected him to hang for a bit. But why would he? Ryker was here to help Honor with her lines, not act as Charlie's companion.

So much for Addie's flirting theory. Her friend was way off.

"Thanks for your help tonight with the lines. That was really smart. She's going to love learning them that way, I think. And carving pumpkins as a reward was a great idea, too. I'm sure we're going to do a lot less fighting about the extra schoolwork now."

"Hopefully it will make it easier on both of you.

You've already done so much for Honor. Adding another thing is a lot to ask."

Charlie shrugged off the compliment. It came with the territory.

"Maybe for the next week's reward, you two can come out to Sunny Farms. Or I can ask Angela for permission to take Honor for the day so we're not monopolizing more of your time."

"I don't mind going." And it wasn't about not trusting the man. Ryker had been talking about his work in such fond terms that Charlie wouldn't mind seeing the place. She also wouldn't mind spending time with Ryker in his element.

She was beginning to fear that her *like* meter regarding Ryker was slipping into the red zone. The one covered in hearts. The last thing Charlie needed was to engage in a lopsided relationship with the man. And she couldn't just be straightforward and ask him if he felt anything for her, because if he said no, that would make the time they spent together with Honor incredibly awkward.

So, she'd do what made the most logical sense. She'd bury anything blooming inside her and focus on what mattered.

Which was Honor. Not herself.

Chapter Ten

Honor drew on the erasable toy board Charlie had gotten her as they drove to Sunny Farms.

In the last week and a half, Honor had done her extra schoolwork with only a hint of complaining, and she'd been looking forward to visiting the horses at her uncle's work for almost as long.

The weather had shifted from cold back to sixty today, which felt balmy with the sun beaming down on them.

Charlie had gotten the convertible out—per Honor's request—instead of driving her more logical FJ Cruiser. They'd left the top on, though, since it wasn't quite warm enough to go without it.

Ryker's shift ended at two, so that's when they planned to arrive. The mountains surrounding the horse farm made for a pretty picture as they rumbled cautiously down the drive, attempting not to kick up too much dust. Would be nice not to have to wash the car when she got home.

After Charlie parked near the front office, Honor scrambled out of the back seat.

Should they head inside to ask about Ryker's whereabouts? Or should Charlie shoot him a text to let him know they'd arrived? She'd given him a heads-up before they'd taken off from town, so he should have an idea as to their ETA.

And then there were the questions that weighed most heavily on Charlie—should she even be here at all? Should she have checked with Angela and let Ryker and Honor have this day to themselves?

Before she could analyze all of *that*, Ryker rounded the corner. When he saw them, his face lit up like he'd found the best gift under the Christmas tree. He wore his Sunny Farms polo along with jeans and boots. Casual and commanding at the same time.

Fine, I admit it. I'm here for myself as much as I am for Honor.

All in all, that sounded like an absolutely terrible plan.

Honor ran in Ryker's direction, and he scooped her up in a hug. Charlie rounded the vehicle slowly, not wanting to interrupt. But then Ryker opened his free arm. Charlie stepped into his side, and he hugged her in greeting, too. Like they were old friends. Like the touch didn't ignite something that sizzled under her skin.

She'd considered removing herself from this day for Ryker and Honor's sake. Now she realized she should have done that for her own preservation.

She was getting far, far too attached. To both of them.

"What do you want to see first?" Ryker let go of Charlie and delivered Honor back to the ground. The girl was wearing an outfit she'd helped pick out online— ankle boots and jeans with a bohemian flowered shirt. Charlie had managed to braid her hair in two French braids while it had still been wet this morning. She could only imagine how curly it would be when they sprang it loose after drying.

"Horses!" There was no hesitancy in Honor's demand. She'd been looking forward to this day for eons in kindergarten years.

They walked toward the stables, a few determined leaves still clinging to the aspens that dotted the mountains.

"It's so gorgeous out." Charlie was here now. She might as well enjoy the day with Ryker and Honor while she had the opportunity.

"It is. It's supposed to turn cold again later this week, so I'm glad we got this in." Appreciation crinkled the corners of Ryker's eyes as they met Charlie's and held. "Thank you for making this work. I know you have a lot going on."

His gratitude was heady stuff, and the buzzing that had started with his simple greeting/half hug notched up.

"Of course. It's been a huge help to have this to look forward to—for Honor."

Despite correcting herself, Charlie still blushed. Yes, she'd been looking forward to today, but Ryker didn't need to know that. The less he realized about her unwelcome, unreturned feelings for him, the better. At this point, Charlie *had* to start letting go of the two of them, but God would have to help her, because she didn't know how to even begin walking that choppy road.

The whole time they'd been discussing Honor and Charlie visiting Sunny Farms, his niece had been planning to ride one of the horses. But now that she was standing face-to-knee with one of the massive animals, her body language had turned fearful, and she'd gone nonverbal.

"You can do this, Hon. Horses are so gentle. I promise you'll be safe."

Her head bounced from side to side so quickly he was surprised it didn't make noise.

Okay, so riding might be pushing things. "Why don't you try just sitting on the horse? He'll stand right here next to us and I won't have him walk. He'll stay still." Ryker couldn't promise that Zeus wouldn't flinch or move a leg, but the horse would stay steady if that's how he was directed.

Honor shook her head again, and Ryker glanced at Charlie for backup. What else should he do or say?

"I'm not sure what to do. You're the horse whisperer, not me." Charlie wore a dark green shirt along with jeans and lace-up hiking boots. Her pretty eyes were heavy with concern. Ryker wanted to swoop close and catch another whiff of her lemony scent. He wanted to stand next to her and hold her hand and have it be the two of them figuring this out. The two of them against the world. Instead, they were *sort of* partners—*sort of* on the same team. "What if you got on the horse and Honor sat with you?"

They watched Honor for a response. Another negative.

Huh. The kids he'd worked with so far who'd come out to Sunny Farms had been gung-ho about riding. Ryker hadn't encountered a situation like this yet, and he didn't know what to do. The whole thing left him feeling inept. If he thought that Honor would go home and not be disappointed that she hadn't ridden a horse, Ryker would let it go in a heartbeat. But she'd been so excited about this. If she didn't try, no doubt she'd regret it.

Charlie stepped forward and ran a hand down Zeus's nose. He was a gentle giant, so Ryker could see why Honor was freaking out. But Zeus would barely snap his tail to dislodge a fly, he was so calm.

"You're a sweet boy, aren't you?" Charlie spoke to the animal, who seemed to bow his head in regal agreement. Honor took a step closer to Charlie, intrigued but still not certain. Ryker picked her up, and she clung to him, wrapping arms and legs around him as he moved next to Charlie.

"I'm not putting you on the horse. I promise I won't do that without your permission, okay?"

Honor gave the slightest nod of understanding, and her hold loosened a centimeter. At least she trusted him.

Charlie squeezed Honor's calf through her jeans-clad leg. "What part scares you the most, Hon?"

She took her time answering, eventually removing her thumbnail from her mouth. "It's so big. What if I fall off? Or it runs away with me?"

They were using the indoor arena since the outdoor was still being used for lessons. It was enclosed. Zeus couldn't take off with Honor, but Ryker was proud of her for voicing her concern.

"This arena has something on all the sides, so he can't run away. And as for falling off, I'm not going to let that happen, either. I'll be right beside you the whole time. If you started to fall, I'd catch you."

It looked as if she was considering what he said but was still uncertain.

Charlie had continued to rub Zeus's nose, talking quietly about how kind and sweet and gentle he was, and eventually Honor reached a tentative hand out to touch him along his neck. Zeus didn't move, and she grew bolder, repeating the petting motion.

"He feels funny. And he has big eyes. And his nose is so hard." She patted him there. "You're a good horsey, aren't you?"

Ryker shared a smile with Charlie behind the girl's back.

Honor's comfort level was growing. She might not ride or sit on Zeus today, but they'd still made progress. They stayed in the same spot for a chunk of time. Honor didn't request to ride Zeus, so Ryker didn't suggest it. His gut told him that pushing would result in more trauma. She'd figure it out in her own timing. Just like school.

Charlie ran her hand along Zeus's neck. "Would it be a lot of work if we stabled Zeus—or whatever you call it and wherever he goes—and toured the rest of Sunny Farms? And then maybe we can come back later if Honor wants to say goodbye to him before we go?"

Honor's head bobbed in agreement with Charlie's plan. Ryker handed the excess lead rope to Honor and kept her in his arms as they walked back to the stables. The whole time Honor kept beaming at Zeus, as if the horse could read her face. Since Zeus seemed to smile back with those soulful eyes, maybe he could.

After situating Zeus, Ryker showed the girls the rest of the place—the stables, barns, various outbuildings. They stopped to watch some of the lessons outside and then ended in the offices.

He introduced them to Lou, who was delighted to meet them both and doted on Honor like a grandmother would. Correction—like any grandma besides Ryker and Kaia's mom would. Oh, Mom loved Honor, no doubt. Liked seeing pictures of her or talking to her on the phone. She just wouldn't go so far as to interrupt her wants with Honor's needs.

"Let me show you something." Lou motioned Honor behind the front reception desk and back to her office. Honor was curious enough to follow her.

Ryker and Charlie stayed where they could see but not interrupt, watching through Lou's office door as she opened a desk drawer and both she and Honor peered inside.

Whatever they studied in there took a minute. Eventually Honor's head popped back up and she held a sucker.

"Lou's famous candy drawer." One of the college-age barn assistants whose name Ryker had completely and embarrassingly forgotten nodded toward the office as she passed by. Man, he was seriously terrible at remembering names. "Many a kid has picked up a treat after lessons."

"Smart." Charlie's brow furrowed. "Why didn't we think of that?"

"We did. Coming out here and getting to ride a horse was supposed to *be* her reward."

"Right? She's been talking about it nonstop."

Ryker had been looking forward to today with the excitement of a kid about to get their driver's license, and not just because of Honor. He'd wanted to show Charlie around, too. Give her a glimpse of what she'd helped bring into existence. He wouldn't be standing here, working here, if she hadn't encouraged him to try.

"Do you think we should push Honor to ride Zeus while she's here? Is she going to be full of regret when you guys get home?"

Lou and Honor were discussing something now, and Honor's cute giggle floated back to them. Maybe Lou would cure the girl of her fears while they were talking.

"I don't know. I wondered the same thing." Charlie scooted a hand through her hair, unleashing a sweet scent. "But my gut also says not to push her. That it might just take some time for her to get comfortable."

"Our guts are speaking the same language. And she can always come back out here—if you're willing, of course. Lou said I was free to ride any time outside of my shifts."

"That's helpful. Maybe she just needs time to adjust. Horses are gigantic compared to her." Lou's laugh sounded through the open office door. "It's great to see Honor talking so easily to someone new. Even without riding Zeus, today has been good for her."

"True." He nudged Charlie's arm with his, not to get her attention, but because his growing need to be near her was currently outweighing his logic. "You always see the positive, don't you?"

She leaned back in surprise. "I do?"

"I think so."

"Well. That's nice to hear. Thanks."

"Did I thank you for bringing Honor out here?"

She laughed. "You did, and you can stop now." She bumped her arm into his this time, and his pulse skyrocketed. Be still his pathetically pounding heart. Ryker would roll his eyes at himself if it wouldn't raise questions from the woman next to him.

Was Charlie flirting with him? And did she even know what she was doing shooting those deep evergreen eyes his way? Somehow, she was oblivious to the fact that she could disarm him with just a look.

And it had better stay that way, because Ryker wasn't sure he'd be able to resist the woman if she figured out how much she affected him.

After they finished the tour of Sunny Farms, Ryker walked to the car with Charlie and Honor.

Despite Honor declining to ride Zeus, the afternoon had been fun. It had given Charlie a glimpse into what "normal" families did together and had only increased her longing for that out-of-reach world.

She'd stepped into fostering because of God's prompting, yes, but also because the desire to be a mother never left her. It was like a birthmark adhered to her skin. She'd craved a child for so long that she'd finally decided maybe the man portion of that scenario wasn't going to happen. So she'd looked into doing things on her own terms. But now that she'd experienced what it was like to have both Honor and Ryker in her life, Charlie didn't want to lose them.

It wasn't just Honor drawing them together anymore. Charlie genuinely liked Ryker.

Too much.

And today, while almost perfect, had left her experiencing that niggling sense of impending loss on repeat.

When they reached the car, Ryker knelt in front of Honor. "You did good today, Hon. Maybe next time we can visit Zeus again." He hadn't said ride. Just visit. Ryker was really good at instinctually knowing how to comfort Honor. How to give her time to figure things out on her own.

"Aren't we going back to see Zeus? I thought I was going to ride him later. Like Charlie said."

Charlie hadn't actually said *ride*, but if Honor had planned on that...

"Is that what you want to do?" Ryker squeezed Honor's little arm. "There's no rush. You can come back another time."

Honor's fingernail slipped between her teeth as she warred with her fears. "I can do it."

If the girl wanted to try, who were they to say no?

The three of them walked back to the stables and repeated the motions from earlier in the day, moving Zeus to the indoor arena. The horse wasn't bothered by any of it, standing calm and strong and stoic, his dark roast eyes full of patience that seemed almost human.

This time when Ryker finished with the saddle, Honor let him lift her up and into it. "Just sit and get comfortable for a minute." Ryker didn't leave Honor's side, keeping his hand on her leg, grounding her. "We're not going to move yet."

She sat tall in the saddle—as tall as a peanut could sit. But while her fears from earlier seemed to have lessened, she still clutched the saddle horn with two white-knuckled hands.

"Tell me what you notice about the place we're in." Ryker's suggestion had Honor looking up and around, her shoulders scooting back.

"It's big. And tall. And no one is in here 'cept us."

"And what about Zeus? What do you notice about him?"

Tentatively one of her hands reached forward. "His hair is soft. Next time I wanna ride a girl with braided hair." Next time. *Good girl.* "Like Charlie braided mine today." Honor preened, sending the braids spilling out of her helmet dancing.

"I noticed that." Ryker tweaked one of her braids. "You look very pretty today, but then, you always do." His smile swung to encompass Charlie, too, turning her stomach to mush. How could such a short glance convey so much? *Thank you. I see you. You're not invisible to me.* If only the words she imagined reading on his face would also come from his lips. Maybe then she could latch on and believe them.

"Okay, I'm ready." Honor was as stoic as if she was going off to battle. Sweet girl. She'd been through so much, and now she was being so brave.

Ryker started them off at a slow walk. Honor teetered a bit in the saddle as she got settled and figured out how to move with the rhythm of the horse. Once the stiffness eased from her body, she looked more confident, more relaxed.

"I'm doing it!" Her near shout was atypical for her, and Charlie clapped and whistled.

"You're doing fantastic, Honor!"

The girl's pride was evident, as was her sheer delight. Zeus had gone from being her nemesis to her best friend in a matter of seconds. She even loosened her hold, using one hand to pat Zeus along the neck and tell him he was doing a good job. The little girl encouraging the massive horse would be comical if it wasn't so tender.

She rode almost thirty minutes before tiring. When Ryker lifted her from Zeus and placed her on the ground, Honor beamed like a switch had been flipped inside her.

Charlie had watched a documentary on the ability of horses to comfort and mimic the emotions of humans. To bring healing in ways that couldn't be measured. Today she'd witnessed it firsthand. No wonder Ryker wanted to work with these magnificent creatures for a living. He'd said horses had saved him when he'd been a teen, and Charlie had thought he'd been exaggerating.

Not anymore.

Ryker's phone rang after they'd cared for and stabled Zeus, so she and Honor walked a few steps ahead of him as he answered.

A lot of *ah-huh*s and *okay*s punctuated his end of the conversation. Charlie's curiosity grew as the excitement in his voice escalated.

"Thanks so much, man. I owe you big-time. I'll have my mom come by and get my stuff out of there. It's the least she can do."

They exited the stables as Ryker disconnected and pocketed his phone.

"Good news, I take it?"

"The best." Ryker scooped Honor up and swung her around in a circle, making her giggle. "Finally rented out my room back in Texas. The guy is moving in next week. I'm going to have my mom pick up my stuff and stick it in her garage so I don't have to worry about it for now. I'm getting my deposit back, and I'll also get my first paycheck from here." He motioned toward the office. "Which means I should be a step closer to getting my own place." He plunked Honor on the ground, and they continued walking.

Ryker didn't explain that his new place would be for him *and* Honor. And it was probably best that they didn't get into those kinds of details with her yet. Not until things were certain. But Charlie knew what the developments meant.

She also knew that this visit to Sunny Farms, which had started out with fear and ended in victory, had suddenly turned bittersweet.

Chapter Eleven

Everything was changing so fast it was giving Charlie whiplash.

In one week, Finn would close on the ranch and officially become a Westbend resident. And tonight, in a move unprecedented before this time, Honor had a playdate.

The odor of degreaser and floor cleaner mingled as Charlie pressure washed the shop floor. Brake fluid spill today. Scott had offered to take care of it, but Charlie had sent him home, needing the distraction.

Never had she imagined she could be nervous for a five-year-old on a playdate.

Charlie paused and retrieved her phone from the pocket of her coveralls. She'd text Addie and see what her friend was up to. If Evan was in town, maybe they could sneak away for a quick girls' dinner.

After sending the message, she returned to the machine.

Why was she so jumpy about this playdate? Honor and Gabby played together at school all the time. If Honor was going to jabber about anyone, it was Gabby. Ironic because of her friend's name. Their relationship had brought out a new side in Honor and broken down her walls.

But what if something changed? What if they got into an argument and it affected their friendship? Or what if Honor didn't feel safe and didn't have a way to let Charlie know? She doubted that last one was possible, or she wouldn't have let Honor go.

"Argh." Charlie gave the cleaner an extra shove over the stained part of the floor. As if her frustrations could be scraped away along with the dirt and grime.

Her phone vibrated in her pocket, and she scrambled for it like someone with a tree-nut allergy lunging for their EpiPen.

I wish we could hang out! I would love that. I miss you. Unfortunately, I have quite a few guests tonight and Sawyer is sick. The text included the green-faced emoji.

Oh no! I'm so sorry. Is it a cold or stomach stuff?

The first plus an ear infection.

That did not sound fun. Is Evan there to help you?

Yep. He leaves tomorrow for a trip, but he's on drink duty right now. We're trying to keep Sawyer hydrated.

I'm glad you have help. Let me know if you need anything—soup, medicine, whatever.

I will, thanks!

Charlie was confident that Addie would notify her if she required assistance. She wasn't overly determined to rule the world on her own like *some people* had a tendency to do.

Not that Charlie was over-the-top in that way. She was okay at accepting help. She just liked to be so organized and efficient that it wasn't necessary.

"Hello?" The call came from the rear shop entrance, and Charlie flipped off the cleaner.

"Back here."

Ryker rounded the vehicle still in bay one, and Charlie's heart dropped and did ten pushups at the sight of him. "Hey. What's going on?" Had he stopped by to see her? Or had he forgotten they'd moved his visitation to tomorrow night?

"You're still working?" He scanned her current situation. "Or…cleaning?"

"Yeah. We had a spill today. Brake fluid."

"Gotcha. Is Honor upstairs then? I didn't see her outside."

So, it was the second option. *I* refuse *to be disappointed it wasn't the first.*

"Remember that we switched nights? Gabby had asked if Honor could come over to play, and this was the only evening they could make work this week."

Ryker scrubbed hands over his face. "That's right. I forgot about the switch. Between work and Alma's news about the duplex, I've been running like crazy."

"Alma's news? Not sure you told me about that."

Ryker's grin flashed, and Charlie's stomach somersaulted. If he stuck around any longer, she'd turn into a gymnast. "The people who had rented her duplex—the one two blocks from here—canceled on her last minute. I guess one of them got a job elsewhere, so they're not staying in town. It's available again, so she called me. Now that my place in Texas is rented and I have a job here, I can actually sign the lease with a clear conscience. And I've got the deposit money. It's perfect timing."

Oh. Ryker's revelation registered like a sucker punch. It was another step toward losing Honor. A big one.

"That's…great. I'm happy for you."

Her tone must have failed to validate her response, because Ryker winced. "Sorry. I know this is awkward."

Get a hold of yourself, Charlie Brightwood. None of this is a surprise.

"It's a good thing that you're making progress. Honor should be with family." Not only did Charlie keep telling herself that, she believed it. The system's goal was to re-unite families if possible. She would never have signed up for fostering if she didn't agree with that objective.

And hopefully once Honor moved in with Ryker, the constant sting would lessen. At least that was her prayer. And prayers were allowed to be big, impossible requests. Figuring out how to lose Honor definitely fit that definition.

"You're being really generous about all of this. I'd be a terrible jerk if I were you."

"What can I say? I'm a really generous person." Of course she was being sarcastic and dousing her emotions with humor, but Ryker, bless him, let her get away with it. "So does tomorrow night still work for a visitation and working on play lines?"

"Yep. I'll make it work."

"Thanks. Now you've got a night to yourself." The very thing that had Charlie stressed out. She'd been on her own for so long and had never cared about doing things single. Movies. Dinner. Travel. Whatever. Didn't matter, she did it. But one month of Honor's presence had somehow changed all that.

"I'll probably go back to my place and pack up what little I have and move it over to the duplex." His forehead creased. "Not sure how I'm going to furnish my new place. The house where I lived in Texas was already furnished when I moved in, so I don't own much there, either. Just a bed and dresser and a few small pieces of furniture that aren't worth going back for right now. I can replace them here for cheaper than the cost of driving and moving the stuff." Ryker raked a hand over the back of his neck. "Guess I'll be sleeping on an army cot for the foreseeable future. But as long as Honor has what she needs, I couldn't care less about myself."

Sacrificial man. Who else would have literally dropped their life in Texas for the sake of their niece and picked up a new one in Colorado without even a pinch of remorse or regret? Ryker Damon Hayes, that's who.

"What about you? What are you going to do with your free evening?"

Pray that Honor's playdate goes really, really well. Charlie glanced around the shop. She was done cleaning. All that remained was storing the machine.

"You're not working tonight, are you?"

"Maybe."

"Are you that far behind still? I thought you and Scott had caught up."

"We're fine. We're pretty caught up, actually."

"So, if you're not working because you're in desperate need...what's going on?"

"I'm trying to distract myself."

"From what?"

Her sigh was extended and embarrassed. "From over-thinking Honor's playdate. I'm not worried about Honor being at Gabby's house. I know enough about Camila to trust that her home is a safe place for her. I'm just apprehensive over how things are going for the girls. Gabby is Honor's only friend, as far as I can tell. There's a lot at stake. I just hope it goes well and they stay friends. That nothing blows up or turns into a fight or anything weird like that."

Ryker's head tilted. "Have you known a lot of five-year-old girls who get into tussles with each other?"

She laughed. "No. But like I said, I didn't have a ton of girlfriends growing up. The relationships I saw always seemed so volatile."

"Sure. And those girls probably have drama mamas. They don't have someone consistent and calm like you or Camila in their lives."

The fact that Ryker considered her a mother figure for Honor registered like a warm, cleansing washcloth after a long, taxing day. Charlie hadn't let herself go there—especially since her time as Honor's foster parent was quickly coming to a close.

"You're cute when you're worried."

Ryker's comment sent Charlie's blood whipping through her veins. What did he mean by that? *He just says things sometimes. Don't overthink it like you are everything else right now.*

But then Ryker's hand skimmed her cheek, and any logic Charlie had just dug deep for grew wings. For the strangest second, she thought he was going to lean close and kiss her. Her lids fluttered shut in anticipation, quickly shooting back open when she realized she must have imagined the moment.

Ryker's hand was back by his side, and her skin screamed silently at the loss.

"Want to help me grab my stuff and then see my new place? It'll distract you."

The place where Honor would live with him. The place that might take both of them away from her.

Ever since her relationship with Ryker had started to change for the better, Charlie had repeatedly beat down the sneaky, backstabbing fear that he was only befriending her because of her link to Honor. And at times, despite her efforts, that suspicion rose back up, vicious and strong and tormenting.

It couldn't be true, though, could it? If that were the case, why would Ryker offer to hang out with her right now when Honor wasn't present? He could tell she needed a distraction, and he was extending an olive branch.

Charlie's instincts said to refuse it. To hole up and handle everything on her own. But she didn't want to be that scared version of herself anymore.

Honor had taken a huge step away from her fear when she'd ridden Zeus.

Ryker had done the same with his when he'd driven out to Sunny Farms to apply.

And now it was Charlie's turn. She had to at least attempt to trust that Ryker's relationship with her wasn't solely about Honor. That their friendship meant something and would continue after Honor changed addresses.

Charlie had to try. She had to believe that she mattered in all of this. Because if she didn't…she wasn't sure she'd ever recover.

Since they'd left Charlie's garage, she had relaxed slightly, but the playdate was still definitely weighing on her. The fact that Charlie cared so much about something as small as Honor playing with a friend only made Ryker more attracted to her. Not an area where he currently required any sort of push.

He was treading awfully close to risky territory, and he couldn't recall why standing at the edge of this cliff was so dangerous. This cliff smelled nice. It had flawless skin that reminded him of peaches. And not only was the cliff pretty, it was funny and kind and generous, too.

Before they'd left her place, Charlie had changed out of her work clothes and into a heather-gray hoodie and jeans with navy blue Converse. She looked cute and comfortable, and Ryker had equal parts wanted to tuck her under his chin and snuggle with her and tug on her sweatshirt until she landed against him. Until those rose lips of hers met his.

Just like he'd been contemplating when they'd been standing in her shop.

He really, *really* needed to get his head on straight. But being with Charlie without a five-year-old to distract him wasn't helping that plan in the least.

Ryker hefted the bag of his clothes he'd just finished packing onto his back. He'd thrown in quite a bit before driving to Colorado because he hadn't known what to expect for weather. Since being here, he'd purchased a few things, and his Texas roommates had shipped a couple boxes of his stuff. Other than clothes, he also had toiletries, food, towels, bedding, his cot.

What did Charlie think of him and his lack of worldly items? And what did it matter? Despite his lapses in judgment tonight, he and Charlie weren't meant for each other.

Besides his refusal to engage with her while his focus remained on Honor, Charlie was way out of his league. She'd grown up in a good family. A loving family. And while Ryker had experienced enough of that to be just fine, he also had a mountain to overcome in the form of family drama.

He wouldn't even be in this town or in the vicinity of Charlie if his sister hadn't lost custody of her daughter.

Outside, Charlie had the passenger door of his truck open, and she was standing next to it. "I got the food packed up."

"Great. Thanks."

"Is that the last of your stuff?"

"Yep." He tossed the bag into the back and climbed into the driver's seat.

The drive to his new place would only take a few minutes. A topic they did not discuss on the way: how close the duplex was to Charlie's. Ryker wasn't sure how she felt about the location, but he didn't plan to ask because he didn't have any other options.

He was actually relieved by the proximity of their places. It would make the switch to kinship care easier for Honor if Charlie was close by and still involved. As much as she was willing to be. It would stink if yet another person was deleted from Honor's life as if they hadn't existed in the first place.

Thankfully he could be confident that Charlie would never let that happen.

When they reached the duplex, they both grabbed items, carrying in everything he owned in the state of Colorado in two trips.

I'm not going to let that stress me out. At least not

tonight. Maybe after he slept it would all feel less overwhelming.

Ryker set up the cot in what would be his bedroom upstairs and then returned to the kitchen to find Charlie unloading the cold food into the fridge.

"You're going to need supplies along with furnishings."

Obnoxious dollar signs flashed in his mind along with the sound of an old cash register—*ka-ching, ka-ching, ka-ching.* Was he crazy to not return to Texas for his stuff right now? But what did he even have there that was of value? Worn towels, clothes and a dresser with two broken drawers weren't worth the trip. Even the bed, which was comfortable but nowhere near new, would take too much time and money to transport. It was better to start over here than to dump his paycheck into moving old things.

She pulled out her phone. "We should hit the thrift store before it closes." She showed him the hours on her screen. "You can do supplies later, because Len's grocery store will be open longer."

They had forty minutes, and a thrift store sounded like a fantastic solution. Much better than holing up in the corner throwing a tantrum.

"Let's do it."

At the thrift store, they searched out half-price tags. Ryker experienced a flash of embarrassment that his current situation required as much but quickly shoved it aside.

Moving at the drop of a hat had been costly, but worth it.

Charlie found him a matching set of blue plates— not a full one, but enough for him and Honor to make do. Ryker snagged some kitchen necessities. They'd be eating at home, of course. It made the most economical sense.

They scavenged until the store closed, and Ryker enjoyed himself far more than he'd expected to while spending money he didn't want to spend.

Charlie offered to drive his truck up while he checked out, so he tossed her the keys. When he grabbed the bags and headed out the door, she'd parked right out front but had switched over to sit in the passenger seat.

He put the dishes in the cab of the truck and the rest in the back and then got in. "What time do you have to get Honor?" It was a school night, so Ryker assumed she wouldn't be over at Gabby's too late.

"Seven. Camila convinced me to let her stay through dinner. She said she'd have them do any homework they had together."

Ryker drove out of the lot. "I assume that means Honor is getting a night off from her extra studies?"

Charlie's lips curved, and Ryker forced his gaze back to the road. The woman's distraction level was on par with texting while driving. "Yeah. I haven't been so crazy about that—not like I was at the start. Just twenty minutes a day and then we call it. It's working, too. She's doing so much better already—at least from what I can tell. We'll see what her teacher says when she has a conference, but I'm excited for her."

"You're pretty amazing, Charlie Brightwood."

She just laughed. Was she ever going to believe anything he said? Charlie was the queen of deflecting.

Ryker's phone rang as he pulled up to the duplex. He tossed the truck into Park and answered as Charlie got out and started gathering bags.

"Hey, Mom. What's up?" Had she heard something more about Kaia? Maybe she'd been in touch with Kaia's father.

"I'm getting married!" Her squeal echoed over the phone, and Ryker winced at the tone and the declaration.

"What? What are you talking about?"

"Arrow asked me to marry him."

Arrow? What kind of name was that? "Mom, I don't even know who you're talking about. I didn't even know you were in a relationship." Correction—he hadn't listened long enough to retain that information. Ryker could admit he'd tuned his mom out over the years when it came to her dating. The woman was like a record on repeat, and never getting to change the vinyl was pure torment.

"I told you about him. Arrow and I started dating at the beginning of September." Which would have been just before Ryker had taken off for Colorado. No wonder he hadn't heard what she'd said about this guy. He'd been busy focusing on Honor's care while trying to figure out what was going on with his sister. How fitting that Mom had spent the time he'd been uprooting his life and turning it upside down in order to take care of Honor focusing on herself.

And falling in love—or whatever she thought this relationship entailed—in a month.

Ryker had a framed view of Charlie through the windshield as she moved bags into his place without interrupting him, though the concerned look she tossed back in his direction before letting herself in through the unlocked door spoke volumes. She cared about him in some way, shape or form. Just like Ryker did for her.

Yeah, maybe he could see how someone could fall

in love in a month. It wasn't impossible. But with his mom, it was stupid. This wasn't her first rodeo. She should know better.

"Don't you think this guy should meet your kids before proposing to you?"

"He couldn't. You were off gallivanting in Colorado, honey."

Gallivanting, meaning attempting to care for his niece. Right. "I'm not off on a fun run, Mom. I'm trying to take over kinship care of Honor because your daughter has disappeared." She gave a huff of offense, but Ryker continued before she could make excuses for her lack of interest in her granddaughter. "Have you heard anything from Kaia's dad? Anything about how she's doing?"

"Why would I talk to that man? I haven't spoken to him in years, nor do I plan to."

Because your daughter's a mess, Mom. She needs you and *her dad. She needs help.* Ryker dropped his forehead to the steering wheel in lieu of letting the words that wouldn't change anything fall from his mouth. *Thanks for reminding me where I came from, Mom. For showing me just what kind of chaos happens when a person only focuses on themselves.*

This was why Ryker had been so careful to keep his relationship with Charlie platonic all along. Because he certainly wasn't going to turn out like his mother and selfishly put himself first.

Even if it killed him not to.

Chapter Twelve

Charlie had carried in everything Ryker had purchased at the thrift store and now didn't know what to do with herself. She peeked through the blinds of the window over the kitchen sink and found that Ryker was still sitting in the cab of his truck. His free hand flailed about every few seconds, as if he was arguing with whoever was on the other end of the line. His mom, if Charlie had heard correctly when he'd first answered.

Was something wrong with Kaia? And should Charlie leave? Ryker had driven her, but she could walk two blocks.

Instead of heading back out the door, Charlie unloaded the dishes he'd purchased into the sink, filling it with hot water. He didn't have dish soap yet. Didn't really have much at all. It made sense considering how he'd dropped everything in order to move and care for Honor.

If only Charlie didn't find his concern for Honor so attractive. She even liked the side of him that had gone bargain thrift store hunting in order to stock his new place. Charlie was careful with money, so it was nice to see Ryker was, too.

Not that you're going to be marrying him or anything, so what does it matter? She rolled her eyes at herself in the empty apartment. *It matters for Honor's sake. It's another plus in the column that says Ryker's going to be a good influence for the girl.*

After the sink was piping hot and full, Charlie flipped off the water. If she didn't think Ryker would take her head off, she would go to the store herself and get him some paper goods and soap.

In the meantime, she unpacked the other items and added the kitchen utensils and silverware to the scalding water. She got out her phone and made a list: *dish soap, dishwasher detergent, laundry detergent*. She scavenged for a washer and dryer, relieved there was a small stacked set on the main level. It would make things much easier for Ryker. Honor went through outfits like a rock star during a performance and somehow managed to get everything dirty even if she only wore it for two minutes.

Charlie continued adding to the list of needs until it overwhelmed her. What would Ryker do when he realized all that was required in order to set up the place? He'd been working so hard to gain the right to care for Honor. This would feel like a setback, no doubt.

It will work out. These things are only physical. And she'd remind him of that when he came inside. *If* he ever came inside.

Charlie checked the time on her phone. She had about thirty minutes before she needed to pick up Honor. Should she start the walk back to her place?

"Hey." Ryker came through the door. "Did you already get everything?"

She nodded.

"I'm sorry about that. My mom. She just—" He groaned. "She drives me crazy. She is crazy. And all about herself." He scanned the room, landing on the sink and the other items she'd unpacked. "But you are not." His anguished comment ended on a sigh, and then he strode across the space and enveloped her in a hug. She was crushed against his chest—wrapped up tight in his arms—and she never wanted out.

He smelled clean and simple. Like he had his own scent that would forever be seared into her memory.

"What would I or Honor do without you? I don't think I've ever met anyone so generous and selfless."

"I think maybe your comparisons are skewed."

Ryker shook with laughter, and his arms tightened for a second. "I don't."

Well. "You say the nicest things to me, Ryker Damon Hayes. You'd better be careful, or I'll get used to it."

He tensed. His hold loosened, and he removed himself from her personal space as if she were an electric fence and he'd been zapped.

Was it what she'd said? Or maybe she had something in her teeth…or she smelled…or—and this option was quite possible—it could be that he'd noticed the ever-present ultrafine layer of hair that lined her upper lip. That must be it. Definitely the lip hair. Didn't matter that she had to use a magnifying glass in order to assist in its removal.

"I should drive you home." Ryker studied the center of her forehead, avoiding direct eye contact. What in the world had just happened? "You have to grab Honor, right?"

"Yeah, I do."

"I'll take you back to your place."

Charlie swallowed a disgruntled snort and a strange rush of emotion that felt an awful lot like…tears. No. No way. She definitely was not going *there*. "I can walk. It's not far." She moved past him to the door.

Ryker didn't reach out to stop her, but he did follow. "Nah. I'll swing you back."

She wanted to say no, but fighting would only prolong things. "Okay." She begged her voice not to wobble. She begged her body to hide her shaky reaction at least until she got home. Once she was behind her closed apartment door, she could call Addie and talk this through with someone who would help her make sense of it.

Only Sawyer was sick, so Charlie wouldn't be bugging her tonight.

A lonely ache turned to ice inside her, and that invisible feeling she'd been buried under for decades resurfaced.

Someday—maybe when she was sixty—Charlie would understand men. Maybe then she'd be able to read their signals or understand mysteries like why Ryker had gone from boiling to freezing just now. Maybe then she'd figure out how to trust that someone could actually love her and not just see her as a cog in their plans.

Because at this moment, it was awfully hard for her to believe that she and Ryker had a relationship that revolved around anything but Honor.

Or that once the girl exited her life, Charlie would ever see either one of them again.

* * *

Ever since the phone call from his mom last week, Ryker had kept himself busy. Keeping busy gave him less time to miss what he couldn't have with Charlie. It also kept him focused on Honor. On getting his place ready for her.

He kept telling himself busy was good, that it created purpose. In truth, busy was lonely.

Over last weekend, Finn had asked Ryker if he could help him move some things into his ranch house. In the spirit of busyness, Ryker had said yes. He'd also said yes because of Charlie. She'd done so much for Honor. It was nice to be able to return the favor, even if he was only helping her brother move.

Finn had tried to pay him, but Ryker had refused any money.

In the end, Finn had persisted in giving Ryker a couch he didn't have room for at the ranch house. Ryker had accepted after some prodding, and the espresso leather monstrosity now filled his living room. He'd also found a small table and chairs that had been for sale locally.

He'd chipped away at the list Charlie had made of what he needed in order to set up his new place, and he was getting close. The biggest, most glaring items left were for Honor's bedroom. Ryker had been on the lookout day and night for some gently used, local furniture that fit his budget, but nothing was right.

Honor loved her room and her bedroom set so much at Charlie's. Ryker wanted to create that same sense of safety and happiness at the new place. He wanted her to *want* to come home. Not to have to. And while the right bedroom set wasn't going to make that happen, it certainly wasn't going to hurt.

Interestingly enough, Angela had finally granted him unsupervised visitations, but despite that, Ryker hadn't seen Honor or Charlie in the last handful of days because of the extra play practices she'd had. He had continued helping her with her lines for the play, though—even if it was over the phone. Honor knew them like she knew her own reflection in a mirror.

She was going to rock tonight.

And yes, Ryker was nervous for her, which was new territory. He could only imagine how Charlie was holding up.

He parked in the elementary school lot and followed the herd of parents heading inside. The weather had turned crazy cold, and Ryker had been forced to purchase a winter jacket. Previously he'd gotten by with his lined flannel, but this cold front wasn't messing around. He'd picked a jacket that would supposedly keep him warm even with below-zero temperatures, though he wasn't sure that was physically possible. When it came to cold weather, Charlie would say his Texas was showing. Underneath he wore a waffle-knit shirt and jeans with his lace-up boots. He'd made sure to check with Charlie about the dress code for this thing, not wanting to show up casual and find out it was the opposite.

Ryker welcomed the rush of warmth when he stepped inside the doors. He planned to hold them open for the next surge of adults, but that plan changed drastically when he recognized Mrs. Robinson—the woman who'd hit on him the night they'd painted sets—a few people back. Her real name was something he hadn't sacrificed brain space to remember. She was all dolled up—wearing super-high heels and bright look-at-me pants that screamed teenager when she was anything but. Ryker would guess she was a chunk of change older than him. And while age didn't matter in the least, behavior did.

Give him Charlie in her Converse, jeans and sweatshirt with her big, generous heart any day of the week.

Ryker released the door like it was causing fourth-degree burns to his hand and faded into the crowd before Mrs. Robinson could spot him.

Inside the auditorium, he paused to scan for Charlie. He spotted the back of her head—her red hair popping against the sea of brown and blond and black. She had texted that she would save him a seat, so he reentered the river of parents cascading down the aisle. Just how massive was this play going to be? Ryker had assumed it was a simple elementary play, but it looked like half the town of Westbend was in attendance.

His nerves surged up another notch. *Honor will be fine. She's prepared for this.*

In truth, she was prepared for her lines. He didn't know if she was ready to walk out on the stage and see all of these people staring back at her. Hopefully Ms. Rana had prepped the kids for that shock. But then, she headed up numerous plays every year, from what Ryker had overheard. Surely she knew what she was doing.

He reached Charlie.

"Hey!" She greeted him with a shaky grin—because of nerves, he assumed—and snagged her jacket from the seat next to her. She wore jeans with ankle boots and a soft-looking camel-colored sweater, and she'd done something to her eyes to make them shimmer and pop even more than normal.

"Hey." Ryker forced his gaze to the stage as he sat and quickly corralled his troublesome attraction to Charlie. He couldn't afford another mishap like the one at his duplex last week. After he'd gotten off the phone with his mom he'd been so upset, so vulnerable. To step inside and find Charlie being Charlie…he'd practically mauled her with that hug.

Her comment about getting used to his compliments had snapped him back to reality. He couldn't lead Charlie—or himself—on. After his mom's latest shenanigan, Ryker was even more determined not to repeat her self-centered mistakes.

"Sorry I'm late."

"You're not. You're fine. I just got here early to save seats, and Honor had to be here ahead of time anyway."

Her knees bounced, and her hands, which were perched on top, squeezed and twisted on repeat.

Ryker reached over, engulfing her two small hands in one of his. "It's going to be okay. She's going to do great. She knows her lines."

Charlie inhaled deeply. She could probably use a few more of those yoga breaths, but Ryker didn't mention that. He wasn't in the business of telling women what to do if he could help it. That usually didn't end well.

"Thanks to you." Charlie's gratitude landed on him and stuck like honey.

He swallowed and fished for words when all he wanted to do was lean over and kiss her hello. Tell her he'd missed her. All things on his *not happening* list.

With texts from his mom about wedding plans coming in at top speeds all hours of the day, it hadn't been that hard to remember why Charlie was off-limits. Why he refused to continue that sort of selfishness for another generation. Why Honor had to come first.

But remembering and following through were two very different things.

Some people would accuse him of being angry over his mom's current actions. They'd be right. There was far too much going on right now with Honor and Kaia for Mom to be acting like she was eighteen instead of fifty-four.

Ryker wanted to reach through the phone and shake her. Make her realize how illogical and immature she was being. But nothing had woken her to that truth in the past. Why should anything be different now?

"I had to do something," he responded to Charlie. "You were handling everything else. The much harder stuff, like extra schoolwork and showering and eating."

Her light laugh raised his spirits, made him feel like a king. By sheer willpower, Ryker removed his hand from hers and then leaned forward to greet the rest of Honor's entourage. He shook hands with Finn, who was on the other side of Charlie, then waved at Addie, Evan and Sawyer, who were down the row and out of his reach.

"Hello-hi!" Sawyer waved big at him. Cute kid. Energetic as all get-out, which should make for an interesting evening.

Ryker settled back in his seat, his voice low enough that only Charlie would catch his question. "Do you think they should sit on the end so that they can get out of the row with Sawyer if they need to?" It was like airplane seating in here, and anyone attempting to scoot down the row would be tripping over feet and limbs.

Charlie's mouth bowed. "I asked them the same thing, but they said it would be fine. Addie's theory is that Sawyer will feel more trapped in the middle—like escape isn't an option."

Huh. Interesting philosophy. Ryker hoped it panned out for them.

Since the program wasn't starting yet, Ryker eased forward again, directing his attention to Finn. "How's the new place?"

"Getting there. Though I'm going to need some manpower since a couple guys left when the Burkes sold. Any chance you're interested?"

Funny. A few weeks ago, Ryker would have jumped on the opportunity. Now he had his dream job. "I'm happy at Sunny Farms, but thanks. I appreciate you asking."

It said a lot that Finn would offer something like that to him. Ryker had assumed Finn didn't really like him when they first met. Either that or he'd been protecting his sister. Ryker understood that. He'd do the same in a weird situation like this. But despite whatever misgivings had been there at the start, the two of them had gotten along well while moving Finn's stuff over the weekend. Almost like they'd known each other for years or would have been friends in a different universe.

A little like how Ryker felt about Charlie. How could five weeks make it feel as if he'd always known her? Especially after how they'd started out.

"I understand," Finn responded. "That's good. A man has to find a place that fits, or we're in for a long haul."

"True." If only Charlie wasn't the first *place* that popped into Ryker's mind.

"How was work today?" Charlie edged in his direction as she asked, and it took everything in Ryker not to pretend he hadn't heard so that she'd scoot even closer and repeat the question.

"Really good. I got to sit in on some interviews for a few students looking for internships." Not that he was the be-all, end-all decision maker by any means, but the fact that Lou wanted him involved with the younger staff was a huge compliment for him. Lou, he was learning, was excellent at directing people toward their passion. When Ryker had told Finn that he was happy at Sunny Farms, it was an understatement. "What about you?"

"Work was good. I was a little distracted because of tonight, but I don't think I messed up anything too badly."

"I doubt that's even possible."

"Oh, you wouldn't believe the mistakes I've caught myself making."

"Yeah, but the fact that you caught them in the first place says it all."

Her eyes crinkled at the corners. "Sometimes you remind me of my granddad."

"Like I'm an old man?"

She laughed. "No. Like you're really supportive and believe I can do anything."

"If that's the case, then he and I are twins."

The soft smile faded from her face, morphing to questions. So many questions. The same ones that had flashed across her features last week when he'd hugged her at his duplex and then scurried back like a wild animal on the run.

The lights dimmed, saving him from delving deeper into what Charlie was thinking and whether it had to do with him. Maybe she was just worried about Honor and the play, and he was overanalyzing.

He leaned in her direction, his mouth near her ear. "I prayed for her, that she wouldn't be nervous and that her part would go well."

"Me, too." Her whisper was their last communication as a hush fell over the crowd.

Sawyer took the opportunity to loudly question why the lights had gone bye-bye, causing a ripple of amusement in the people surrounding him. Addie shushed him, and Ryker shook with silent laughter.

Yep, this should definitely make for an interesting night.

Chapter Thirteen

Honor—or Lily Lollipop, since she was currently in character—held out her hand to the slightly older girl playing Carmony Candy as she delivered her next line. "Everyone should have a friend. I'll be yours if you need one." Her voice rang loud and clear. No one would know the struggles she'd been through in the last month based on her performance. Ryker had heard Honor say the line more times than he could count, but tonight it was so poignant and fitting—for her and everyone in the audience—that Ryker had to swallow past the emotion that jumbled and stalled in his throat.

Charlie sniffled next to him, as if fighting the same. She won the battle, but from his peripheral vision, Ryker concluded that Addie had not fared so well. She dug in her purse for a tissue, swiping underneath her lashes and then quietly blowing her nose.

Evan looped an arm around her and whispered something in her ear, and she leaned against him as if he was her rock. In the short amount of time Ryker had spent with them—and from what Charlie had told him—he'd been able to discern that the two of them made a good team. They were there for each other in a world where that was incredibly hard to find. And he wasn't sure which of them adored Sawyer more—a testament to Evan, since, according to Charlie, he'd only met the little guy last spring.

The play continued, and after one girl gave a hilarious performance as the tree that couldn't grow leaves, Charlie whispered in his ear. "That's Ruby Wilder. I think she's in the other kindergarten class, but I wish she was in Honor's. Addie says she's a sweetheart." She pointed out a row of people sitting up and to their left. "Those are her parents and aunts and uncles." Seemed Ruby had her own personal fan club, too.

Ryker counted down lines with each one that Honor said. When she recited her last one, he let go of a breath he hadn't realized he'd been holding. Even though he'd been the one to encourage Charlie that they needed to let Honor dream, he'd still been worried that things could implode or backfire at any time. And Charlie had been right—the last thing Honor had needed was any more pain.

When the play finished, the kids all filed onstage—including the backstage crew—and bowed to a standing ovation. Honor waved to the group of them, and the whole lot of them waved back, including Sawyer. They were a besotted bunch if there ever was one.

She bounced on the balls of her feet, her smile megawatt.

Kaia should be here for this.

But if Honor hadn't been taken from his sister, would she even be onstage right now?

Unlikely.

Along with the rest of the crowd, they filed out into the aisle.

"I'll grab Honor," Charlie piped up. "We're supposed to pick her up backstage, and Ms. Rana wants them checked out so that no one gets lost in the shuffle."

"I'll go with you," Finn offered before Ryker could say the same, so he stayed with the rest of Honor's fan base while Charlie and her brother scooted through the crowd.

"I hafta go potty." At Sawyer's announcement, Addie clapped.

"Good job, bug!"

"I'm on it." Evan grabbed the boy's hand, and they dodged through people, weaving their way to the exit.

"Looks like Evan's done this before."

Delight sparked on Addie's face. "Right? He's a natural." Her deep brown eyes shimmered with moisture as she watched him with her son, a backstory Ryker didn't know and wouldn't ask about residing there. "Potty training is no joke. So far we've had more accidents than successes."

"I don't doubt you, nor am I ready to find that out." He understood her need to change the subject, and yet… "You okay?"

She waved off his concern. "I'm fine. I never used to cry this much. I like to tell Evan that it's his fault. It's like he opened up this vault in me and now I'm a waterfall. It's just…when you've been through something hard and actually get to come out on the other side… I tend to be overly grateful for each day. For Evan. For how he loves Sawyer. Basically, what it comes down to, Ryker, is that I've turned into a bumbling sap."

He chuckled. "I wouldn't say bumbling."

"Ha! I would be more offended if it wasn't true. Honor did so great tonight. To see her succeed like that was pretty amazing."

"I agree. It is incredible what she accomplished with what she's been through. I was prepared for her to at least forget a line or speak too quietly to be heard, but she was a champ and proved my concerns wrong. Thank you for being here. I know it will make her night to have her own personal cheering section. I'm embarrassed that my family—" His head shook. "What is wrong with them? How are they so messed up that not only did Kaia lose custody, but her dad and our mom aren't even involved in Honor's life?" Frustrated air rushed from his lungs. "Sorry. Didn't mean to dump all that on you."

"You're not dumping. I came from a tough family. We always struggled to get along and then went through some really hard stuff while I was in high school. I know where you're coming from. It's not just circumstances that Honor has to get through. It's also family."

"Exactly. Thank you for putting that into words."

"Charlie hasn't been through that kind of family drama, so sometimes I think she won't understand. But she's fantastic at listening and not judging. I've never had a friend like her before."

"That's what she says about you."

"Aw." Addie beamed. "She's been one of the best things that happened to me when I moved to this town."

"Me, too." Ryker's head shook. "I never would have thought with how things started that we'd end up here."

"You mean that you'd end up falling for her?"

His jaw unhinged. That wasn't at all what he meant. Addie grimaced. "Sorry. Are you still trying to pretend that hasn't happened? My bad for bringing it up, then."

After his shock faded, Ryker laughed. What else could he do? Then he grew serious. "That family stuff we were just talking about—my mom always put her boyfriends first. They mattered more than the welfare of her children. And really, that's how Honor ended up in this situation, too. My sister did the same thing. Her boyfriend introduced her to meth, and it was downhill from there."

Addie's eyes softened and saddened. "I'm sorry. That's incredibly hard and heartbreaking." She touched his arm sympathetically before letting her hand fall away. "But what does that have to do with you? I don't understand."

"I can't follow in those footsteps. I can't make the same mistakes my mom did—and is still doing—and that my sister repeated."

"Ryker, if you're saying that you have to be careful not to develop feelings for Charlie because that would make you like your mother, you're crazy. If you're honest with yourself, you'll be able to admit that you've already been falling for her this whole time. You already *have* feelings. And have they detracted from your relationship with Honor? Have they made her situation worse? I'd say no. If anything, having both of you on her team has made things better. You balance each other out." She paused to reload while Ryker's world tipped on its axis. "Can you name one time that you and Charlie working together, being together, caring for Honor together, has been detrimental to her in any way?"

His mouth flopped open. "I—" Ryker didn't know what to say. He'd just assumed that any romantic relationship would take the focus away from Honor. That no relationship was the only acceptable answer. He'd never factored into play how much better he and Charlie were together or that Honor would actually benefit and not suffer if they took that leap.

All of his mom's choices had been terrible. And Charlie was the complete opposite of terrible.

Sawyer and Evan returned just as Honor, Finn and Charlie rejoined the group. There was a collective celebration as everyone chimed in to tell Honor how well she'd done and how great the play had been—her role in particular.

Honor beamed under the praise as Ryker processed what Addie had said. If he'd been wrong all of this time, it would be the best news he'd ever received. Because then he could stop trying not to fall for Charlie…and let himself feel what had been there all along.

Charlie entered her apartment with a still-bubbling Honor talking—yes, talking—a mile a minute. About the play, the kids in the play, her friends who came to watch her.

It was like something had broken loose inside her, and Charlie hadn't gotten a word in edgewise the whole drive home. She was okay with that. Very okay.

She left the door unlocked for Ryker, who was headed their way. Charlie had gotten a small dessert to celebrate Honor's play. They would have made a fuss over her performance no matter how it had gone, but Honor had done so amazingly well that Charlie wished she had also ordered a singing telegram, a marching band and a ball full of confetti to drop from the ceiling.

As it was, the small chocolate cake from the local bakery in town would have to do.

Honor ran to change into her pajamas. Charlie would be doing the same if Ryker wasn't stopping by. But it was important for both of them to celebrate the girl. Especially since her care would soon be transferring over to him fully. Possibly by tomorrow.

Angela had called today and explained to Charlie that she'd planned a home visit with Ryker tomorrow. Barring any unforeseen issues, they'd move Honor right after because Angela's supervisor wanted the case moved to kinship care as quickly as possible.

She'd thanked Charlie for doing all that she had for Honor and had said she'd wanted to prepare her.

Charlie appreciated that, but she'd been preparing for this for weeks and the confirmation hadn't made anything easier. While she was thankful she could trust that Ryker would provide a safe, caring, nurturing home for Honor, that didn't stop the wave of sadness that had toppled her. Since that conversation had happened earlier today—before the play—Charlie had attempted to put it aside and enjoy the night.

For the most part, her plan had worked.

"Hello." Ryker gave a quick knock as he poked his head inside the door. "Where's our shining star?"

"I'm right here!" Honor flew out of her bedroom, twirled then bowed.

"Good thing all of this hasn't gone to your head." Charlie's comment earned laughter from Ryker.

He latched the door behind him. "You did so great tonight, Hon. I'm really proud of you."

"Thank you." She grinned at her uncle and then scooted over to Charlie. "Did you say there was celebration cake?" Between Charlie and Addie, they were training her well that all successes ended with dessert.

"There is. Ryker, do you want to work on cutting that while I take off Honor's stage makeup?"

He did as she'd asked, getting a knife out and adding the cake, which was on a small piece of cardboard, to a larger plate so that the crumbs wouldn't go everywhere. Smart man. Now if he'd just load the dishwasher like she did, he'd be close to perfect. Amusement surfaced at her silent joke.

Charlie grabbed a makeup-remover wipe from the bathroom and returned to find Honor sitting on the breakfast bar, telling Ryker about a little boy who'd thrown up backstage during the play.

"Ms. Rana says he wasn't sick. She says it was stage fright." Her pupils tripled in size, as if stage fright was a monster that lived under the bed and came out to prey on young children.

"Stage fright is just nerves in your tummy over doing something in front of a crowd." Charlie gently wiped Honor's cheeks. "I'm sure Ms. Rana was right."

"I'm glad I didn't have it."

"Me, too," Ryker declared. "Sounds messy."

Honor giggled. "It was!"

"Ew." Charlie's nose wrinkled as she paused her ministrations. "Close your eyes," she directed Honor.

The girl followed orders, and Charlie cleared the liner from her little lids. It had seemed overkill to put makeup on a five-year-old, but in the land of theater, Charlie was a novice and had succumbed to the suggestion of another mom who'd said it was normal and would make her look less washed out under the stage lights.

"Cake is served." Ryker placed a plated piece next to Honor along with a fork. It was as large as her head.

"Feeling generous, I see." Charlie shot him a *what are you thinking?* look.

"What? She did such a good job."

Her exhale was part humor, part exasperation. Honor would probably bounce off the walls after all that sugar. And Charlie didn't even want to imagine how bedtime would go.

"Just a small one for me, please."

Ryker's cheeks creased. "That just leaves more for me and Honor." They high-fived.

Honor ate her cake while still sitting on the breakfast bar, and Charlie and Ryker sat on the stools facing her. The three of them chatted about anything and everything while Charlie fought back tears over the changes that were about to happen.

It was late when they finished their desserts. Honor yawned three times before Charlie put the kibosh on the fun and sent her off to brush her teeth.

After brushing, she returned and requested that Ryker put her to bed, so Charlie cleaned up the kitchen while he did.

See? They're already fine without me. Honor will transition to the new place with Ryker just fine. Everyone will be fine. Including me. Somehow.

Ryker returned to the kitchen and leaned against the counter watching her. It was unnerving.

"What?" The word snapped too much. Showed too much.

"What's on your mind?"

"Did you talk to Angela today?"

He nodded slowly, eyes sorrowful. "She's coming by tomorrow after work."

Which meant Charlie had a night and part of a day to figure out how to handle this. Why was it so hard? From the start, the situation with Honor had been something that could fluctuate and change quickly. So maybe her struggle also had something to do with Ryker and the idea that she was losing them both. She'd always planned on—or at least tried to plan on—losing Honor. Not that the measures she'd taken made it hurt any less. But Ryker had been a complete surprise, and she wasn't prepared to find out the truth regarding his feelings. Wasn't ready to know if she'd just been part of the plan—a means to an end—or something more.

Normally she would ask, but she was afraid of the answer.

"Are you ready for the home visit?"

"I think so. The only issue is that I don't have furniture for Honor's bedroom yet. I'd been waiting to find something that she'd be excited about since she loves her set here so much. But now I wish I would have just picked out something. Anything. I'm not sure what Angela will say if her room's not ready. And I have to work tomorrow, so it's not like I can remedy the situation then."

"I'm sure Angela will understand." Charlie's voice broke on the encouragement, and Ryker pushed off the counter, shifting toward her.

Without asking, without thinking, she stepped into his arms. He held her tight, running a hand over her hair. "It's going to be all right."

You don't know that.

Ryker didn't let go of her fully, but he eased back,

his Adam's apple bobbing. He looked as if he wanted to say something more. Instead, his lids closed and his forehead dropped to hers. They stayed that way for a minute, just holding each other while Charlie turned to mush. His hands cradled her face, his thumbs gliding across her cheeks…and then the pad of his thumb traced her lips. Her lungs forgot how to do their job as she contemplated the implications of the ledge they stood on. They could move back now and things would even out, stay safe. Or they could jump together. Charlie voted for door number two. She wanted to kiss Ryker. She wanted to pretend that whatever this thing was between them was real…even if it wasn't. When she went up on her tiptoes, Ryker met her halfway. The kiss was heated and impatient and somehow gentle at the same time. Like the various layers of the man.

Charlie hadn't allowed herself to wonder what it would be like to kiss Ryker because she'd been trying so hard not to go there. Well, she was far beyond *there* in this moment.

She let herself fall, and Ryker urged her closer, until she wasn't sure where she ended and he began. But she did know with certainty that she didn't want any of this to end.

Sadly, it did exactly that. Ryker ebbed back, fingers still tangled in her short locks, eyes hooded. He dropped a kiss to her nose, her eyelids, and she melted like butter on a hot summer day.

"I can't sleep."

At the sound of Honor's voice, they leaped apart like teenagers caught in a forbidden tryst. She was standing in the hallway, squinting against the bright living room light. It was likely she hadn't deciphered what they'd been up to, and if she had caught any of it, she didn't say anything.

"I need you to read me a story."

Charlie swallowed to bring moisture into her barren mouth. "Okay. One story and then you close your eyes and rest."

Honor nodded in agreement.

"This is your fault, you know." Charlie dared to include Ryker in her line of vision. "You're the one who gave her the huge piece of cake." *You're the one who just destroyed me with that kiss.*

"You're the one who bought the cake to begin with." His raised eyebrows and saucy grin seemed to be adding *and you're the one who started the kiss.* Had she? Charlie wasn't sure. Right now she could barely recall her middle name. And Ryker certainly hadn't resisted if she had been the initiator. "I'll go so Honor can get some sleep." He held Charlie's gaze for an extended moment before swooping over to hug Honor once again. "Good night, girls." The click of her apartment door confirmed his departure—and that she hadn't just dreamed up the whole scenario.

Charlie followed Honor into her bedroom and re-tucked her in. She picked up the book Honor wanted and absentmindedly read while her mind stayed otherwise occupied. What had that kiss meant? Did Ryker want a relationship with her after Honor was no longer in her care? Or had the kiss simply happened without prior contemplation?

He hadn't reacted like it had been a mistake, but then, with Honor's appearance, there hadn't been time for a discussion.

When she finished the book, Honor was asleep, dark lashes resting against soft cheeks.

The tears Charlie had been fighting ever since the phone call from Angela sprang into existence. She hoped with everything in her that Ryker had meant that kiss. That tomorrow's home visit and subsequent approval for Ryker to take over Honor's care was the beginning—for all three of them—and not the end.

Because Charlie wasn't sure how she'd survive if it wasn't.

Chapter Fourteen

Ryker could not have picked a worse day to be late.

If he'd left work exactly on time, he would have been fine. But Lou had stopped him on his way out, and one minute had turned into ten.

Now he was flying home to meet Angela at his place while trying not to speed. *She can't take Honor from you because you're five minutes late.* But she could give up on him and leave before the meeting even took place.

He was tempted to call Charlie and ask if she could buzz over to his duplex and stall Angela for him. But that would be a strange request, and Charlie had already done enough for Honor and for him. He had to handle this part, at least, on his own.

After the meeting, he planned to figure out a way to see Charlie and find out what she was thinking. And hopefully not regretting. Ryker didn't harbor any objections over their kiss. Only the desire to push repeat.

All this time he'd been petrified of imitating his mother's mistakes, but as Addie had pointed out, the situations were night and day different. Ryker had been falling for Charlie since he'd arrived in Westbend, and those growing feelings hadn't made things worse.

He'd been about to discuss their relationship with her last night, but then Honor had come out of her room and any chance for conversation had been cut off. Ryker had been impatiently waiting all day to see Charlie and read her face. To know what she wasn't saying in order to know what she truly felt.

Charlie would tell him, even if her words didn't.

When he pulled into the duplex parking lot, Angela was waiting for him.

He popped out of his truck. "Sorry about that. My boss stopped me on my way out of work and it put me behind."

"Not a problem." Angela's eyes were kind, but they weren't warm. Ryker hadn't realized there was a difference until his niece was on the line.

He opened the duplex door and motioned for her to go first.

She paused before entering. "Was that locked?"

Oh man. He definitely was not starting out on a good note. "Ah, no. I'm out of the habit because it's a small town." *And because I don't own anything of value.*

"That's going to have to change if Honor's living here."

"Yes, ma'am." He'd get three locks if it would help. "I'll make a point of locking it from now on."

They stepped inside.

Ryker had picked up last night when he'd gotten home. Not a hard job because of his lack of worldly goods. The place wasn't fancy. It had a '70s vibe, but it was clean.

Angela sat at the table, so Ryker did the same. She

asked questions, made notes and didn't give him any inkling as to what was going through her mind. His nerves were strung tight with no signs of calming.

"Could I have a tour of where Honor will be sleeping?"

"Of course." Ryker's rib cage constricted as he stood. He'd just have to explain to Angela why it wasn't furnished yet, and hopefully that wouldn't keep Honor's care from transferring to him. Someone at work had given him a futon they were getting rid of, and Ryker had been sleeping on that. If he moved it to Honor's room, she'd at least have a bed. But would it be enough?

They walked upstairs. "Honor's room will be on the right." Ryker opened the door to Honor's bedroom and ground to a halt. It was fully set up—with the bedroom furniture Honor used at Charlie's. Even down to the bedspread she loved. How was that possible?

"Everything okay?"

"Yep." Ryker scooted to the side and motioned Angela forward while his mind reeled and spun. How and when had Charlie managed this? She must have done it while he was at work today. To think that she'd sacrificed in this way for Honor—and for him—was more than he could comprehend right now.

"Ryker, did you hear me?" Angela had paused in the middle of the room.

"No, I'm sorry. Could you repeat what you said? I seem to be a little distracted today."

"It's okay." Angela truly softened now, giving him a glimpse of who she was outside of a job that was likely incredibly taxing. "This has been a lot. I understand that. And I'm glad you followed through on all that you did. We want Honor with family first, so this is a win." Her smile faltered. "As much as any situation like this can be considered that. I spoke to Charlie earlier today, and she's planning to bring Honor and her things over when I call her. If you're ready, I'll step outside and do that."

"You mean that's it? It's final? Just like that?"

"Just like that after you've been working toward this for over a month."

"Wow. I'm in shock."

"It moves quickly sometimes, especially when things are in order like you have them. You've proven yourself, Ryker. And my supervisor wants this case moved to kinship care pronto."

"Okay, great." Except he sounded wooden. After all this time, he hadn't expected things to move so suddenly.

Was Charlie okay with this? She had to be if she'd donated Honor's bedroom furniture to her new room.

Within fifteen minutes, Charlie and Honor arrived. He and Angela met them outside.

Honor had been briefed about everything, obviously, because she gave him a big hug. "I'm going to live with you, Uncle Ry. And Charlie's still going to be my friend."

He swallowed twice, attempting to kick-start his vocal cords, then finally just nodded. Honor skipped inside, and Angela went with her, carrying her things... and rolling her bike alongside, too.

Only Charlie. Ryker fought a rising tide of emotion once again.

But the woman who'd done so much, given so much, stayed by her vehicle, one hand on the door as if she might jump back inside at any second.

"Aren't you coming in?"

Charlie's head shook.

When he took a step toward her, she raised her palm. "No. Stay. You need to make this about Honor right now, and I get that."

She was right, of course, but still. "I can't believe you moved the furniture." Gratitude clogged his throat. He wanted to go to her, kiss her, hug her, thank her, but she was right. Honor needed to get settled. And Angela was still here. "I'll call you later tonight."

Why were her eyes so sad? Was the distance tricking him?

"Yeah, okay."

Yeah, okay? What did that mean? Was she second-guessing them or their kiss? Or was it sadness over losing Honor? She wasn't going to lose Honor or him. Not if Ryker had anything to say about it. Not if she was willing to stay in their lives.

"You're going to do great with her, Ryker." Those same eyes that were playing tricks on him glistened. Before he could move closer and confirm tears, she escaped into her FJ Cruiser and backed out of the spot, tearing out of the lot like the police were on her tail.

What was that about? It had almost looked as if Charlie had been saying goodbye just now instead of *See you later* or *We'll talk soon*.

Ryker reentered the duplex. For the moment, he needed to deal with Angela and focus on getting Honor settled and comfortable.

And then he'd deal with the woman he loved—yes, loved—tonight.

It had only been an hour since she'd dropped Honor at Ryker's, but Charlie's apartment had never felt so empty. She passed by Honor's room with a full laundry basket and paused to shut the door. It was too hard to see it without her things in it. Without her.

It will be fine. She will be fine. I will be fine. She'd repeated the mantra over and over again in the last hour.

So far it had failed to come true.

Maybe when Ryker called, every breath she took would stop mimicking the sensation of swallowing fire. Once she talked to him, she could stop worrying and wondering if he cared about her or if everything he'd done had been about gaining the right to raise Honor.

When she'd been at his place dropping off Honor, Charlie had known that if he got too close to her, he'd see the way she'd fallen fast and hard for him scrawled across her features.

And she couldn't go there. Not without some confirmation from him.

A kiss didn't equal a relationship. Charlie had been kissed before and it had amounted to nothing when she'd thought it meant something. But with Ryker and Honor, she craved the real deal. And she was so afraid she wasn't going to get them that she was a mess. She'd never been so undone before. She should call someone. Addie. Finn. She should talk this through with someone, but she couldn't.

She just couldn't.

Taking Honor's beloved bedroom set over to Ryker's today with Scott and setting it up had been about Honor, yes. But it had also been for Ryker. She hadn't known what Angela would do or decide if Honor's room didn't even have a bed in it. And Charlie had known it was time. Time for Ryker to step in and for her to step back.

Moving the furniture had felt a little like yelling from

the roof of her building for all the town of Westbend to hear that she cared not just for Honor, but for Ryker, too. And if he didn't contact her after Angela left...then she had her answer.

About whether he wanted her in his life and Honor's. About the kiss. About how he truly felt regarding her. About all of it.

Charlie started the washer and folded the clothes from the dryer. She'd thought that she'd packed all of Honor's things, but she found a shirt and a pair of socks that were hers hiding in the clean clothes.

No way am I going to cry over socks.

After getting out a bag and placing the items inside to be delivered later, she moved her attention to the dishwasher. When that was finished, she began cleaning out her cupboards, discarding things she no longer used.

She should set the items aside for Ryker. He might appreciate them.

Or maybe I'll never hear from him again.

Enough with the melodrama!

Every time her phone beeped with a notification, she jumped. Every time it wasn't from Ryker, her heart nosedived to her toes.

Maybe they'll walk over once they get Honor and her things situated.

When it slipped past Honor's bedtime, that theory flew out the window.

Maybe he'll call now that Honor's in bed.

When her phone did finally ring, Charlie lunged for it. The screen was filled with Addie's sassy mug.

She didn't swipe to answer until the last second. "Hey."

"How's it going? Are you okay? Do you need company and chocolate?"

"It's going okay." Liar. "I'm fine." Another lie. "And I think I'm okay on the company. I just want to be alone." That last one was the truth. If Charlie saw anyone right now—especially Addie—she'd give the definition of ugly cry new meaning.

"You're a terrible liar, Charlie Brightwood."

Charlie laughed but it ended on a groan.

"Why don't you just tell the man how you feel? He's crazy about you."

"You don't know that."

"Oh, honey. I do. I mean, he pretty much admitted as much last night at the play. There's the faintest possibility I'm mistaken, but I really don't think so. He's like a notebook in high school with your name doodled all over it."

It was easy for Addie to assume, because if she was wrong, it wouldn't annihilate her.

"He said he was going to call. If he does—"

"When he does."

"*If* he does, then we'll talk. Then I'll know what he's thinking. But this is his perfect opportunity to get out, Addie. He *had* to befriend me while I had Honor. It only made sense for us to get along. But now he can have her without me, and maybe that's what he's been waiting for."

Addie's exasperation reverberated in Charlie's ear. "When are you going to trust that someone can and does love you for exactly who you are? That someone *sees* you?"

"When someone proves that to me."

After they hung up, Charlie went back to her cupboards, purging and organizing, wishing she had the control to do the same in her life. But right now, the answers weren't up to her. She'd played her hand with the bedroom set.

Now it was Ryker's move.

At eleven thirty, Charlie turned off her phone and crawled into bed. When she woke up the next morning after a stilted night of sleep and turned her phone on, there were no messages or missed calls from Ryker.

Addie had texted, though. If he doesn't call, I believe there's a good reason. Try to trust that.

So Charlie tried. She tried while she made coffee and got dressed. She tried in the hour before Honor would have gone to school. In the hour after school started.

But she still didn't hear from Ryker.

Her doubts and concerns, which had been vying for attention during the whole fostering process, ignited as if they'd been doused in kerosene.

She'd wanted an answer regarding Ryker's true feelings for her. Now she had it.

It was time to stop hoping that she'd hear from him, that he would have a good explanation like Addie said. If Ryker had wanted to contact her, nothing would have stopped him from making that happen.

So Charlie would bury her hope ten feet underground and then forget it had ever existed.

Because hope, she'd learned, was the scariest thing of all.

Ryker was caught in a nightmare that he feared he'd helped wish into existence. But in all of his prayers asking for protection for his sister—and to know her whereabouts—he'd never expected her to show up on his step unannounced.

Once Angela had left last night, it had taken him a while to get Honor comfortable in the new place. They'd played a game and then built a fort in her room. When she'd gone down for the night, he'd read to her until she fell asleep so that she didn't lie awake for hours combatting loneliness or worries.

After, he'd walked into the living room to hear a knock at his door.

Charlie had been his first and only thought. He'd ripped open the door, his pulse thundering, but it hadn't been Charlie standing on his step. A remorseful, worn version of his sister had been there instead.

I'm sorry to just show up like this. When my dad asked for your address…this was why. I had to know if Honor was doing okay.

Milton Delaney had claimed he'd had something to send for Honor. Ryker should have known the request had more behind it than that.

Kaia had invited herself in.

Ryker hadn't let her wake or see Honor, much to her upset. But he'd been determined not to break any rules. They'd spent the next *three* hours talking. Until Ryker had been so exhausted that he'd almost fallen asleep sitting up.

You can't stay here, Kaia. I have to talk to Angela and make sure you're—we're—following the rules. I'm not about to lose Honor when I just got her. You have to stay somewhere else.

She'd been upset, but she'd understood. Kaia told him her dad had paid for her to go straight to rehab over the last month. She had asked him not to say anything regarding her whereabouts because she'd been afraid that she wouldn't be able to kick the addiction. She'd wanted to get clean first.

I'm working on getting better, Ry. And not just by quitting. There's obviously something deeper going on, and the counselors at rehab helped me start chipping away at that. I feel raw and exposed, like my every issue is visible, but I'm doing it for Honor. I might not believe I'm worth it right now, and I'm working on that, but Honor... She'd broken down then. *She's worth it.*

Ryker had promised Kaia that he'd help her attempt to gain back custody of Honor.

He didn't know what that looked like. How long it would take. Any of it. But he'd said he'd support her efforts. Ultimately, if Kaia could get herself together, it would be the best scenario for Honor. And Ryker didn't have any plans to leave the state or his niece, even if Kaia did accomplish her goal of reuniting with her daughter.

Around midnight, Ryker had sent Kaia over to the room he'd previously rented. His month went through Sunday, so it was still his for now. He sent her with his cot, a blanket and a pillow.

This morning, the first thing he'd done was contact Angela. He'd had to leave a message. Then he'd gotten Honor off to school. After, Angela had called him back requesting that he and his sister come in.

It had pained Ryker considerably to ask Lou if he could be an hour late to his shift. He'd explained the situation, trying to downplay the circus that was currently his existence. She'd said yes, and he'd spent a chunk of time talking with Angela and his sister. Much like Angela had done with him, she'd laid out a plan for Kaia to earn her rights back. It would take time, but the fact that she'd been in rehab—even though she hadn't told anyone—did bode well for her.

Now, Ryker was on his way to Sunny Farms. His body felt as if he'd been hit by a train, he could barely keep his lids from drooping due to lack of sleep and he missed Charlie. His plan had been to convince her to come over last night after Honor was asleep so that they could talk, but Kaia had stolen that from him.

He called Charlie while driving, and the phone rang until it went to voice mail. "Hey, I'm sorry about last night. It was… I can't even begin to describe what all happened." Exhaustion stole his words. "Call me when you can, although I'll be at work, so I might have to talk to you later. Hope you did okay last night." *Love you.* Thankfully he didn't tack on that addition. He'd much rather tell her that in person, when he could gauge her response and read her face…and maybe even hear the same in return.

By the time his break rolled around and Ryker ate the sandwich he'd packed, Charlie still hadn't returned his call.

Strange. Though he had said he would be at work.

He texted her. You okay? I'm on a break. Have time to talk?

When his break ended and he still hadn't heard from her, Ryker shoved his phone in his pocket and went back to work.

He got home in time to meet Honor at the bus stop. Her pickup/drop-off hadn't changed from what it had been at Charlie's. Another consistency that was appreciated. The less change the girl had to handle, the better.

Ryker's shoulders dropped ten inches when she

stepped off the bus. He hadn't realized he'd been harboring concern that Kaia would do something stupid like go by Honor's school to try to see her, or even attempt to pick her up.

Honor ran in his direction, hugged him and then chatted about her day as they walked. She told him about Ruby—a new friend that she and Gabby had made at recess.

"Is she the one who had that funny part in the play? From the other kindergarten class?"

"Yep. We only see each other on the playground, but we played house and princess and it was lots of fun."

"That's great, Hon. I'm glad you made another friend."

Charlie had said Ruby was a sweet kid, so she'd no doubt be ecstatic over the news. The woman was so concerned about Honor making friends, keeping friends. Ryker would tell her about the new development if she ever responded to him.

After dinner, Ryker texted Charlie again. He was starting to worry that something was wrong. It was really unlike her to not answer back quickly.

Once he crashed into bed, he reached for his phone to send another text. But the number of times he'd contacted Charlie without a response stared back at him.

She doesn't want to talk to me.

She was avoiding him. But why?

Because you're a no-good piece of trash. Ouch. The Bruce-ism stung like a rusty nail through his bare foot.

Charlie didn't think of him like that, though. She'd encouraged him. She believed in him.

Then why hasn't she responded?

Was she done with him because her fostering duties

were over? But then why had she kissed him? Charlie wouldn't have done that if she didn't feel something for him. It wasn't in her nature to be flippant about a kiss.

Except…maybe she'd just been caught up in a moment. Maybe she didn't care for him in *that* way. And now she was distancing herself so that he'd figure that out.

Charlie was incredibly direct, and she'd never told him outright she was interested in having a relationship with him. She'd never accepted any of the compliments he'd sent her way. Maybe she'd been trying to show him all along that she wasn't into him like that.

Why had Ryker ever thought that Charlie would go for someone like him? He'd always known he wasn't good enough for her. She was put together, successful, a pillar in the community. He was a glorified ranch hand with a messed-up family. Even as a kid, Charlie had been focused. While she'd been rebuilding a car with her granddad, Ryker had been in survival mode, using all of his energy to disregard the labels and verbal abuses burned into his skin.

So…he'd been right all along—he should never have gone *there* with Charlie. Should never have let things progress beyond friendship.

For a second, Ryker had started to believe that he could have Honor *and* Charlie. That God had orchestrated a partner for him who was beyond anything he'd ever imagined deserving. But he should have remembered the truth of his childhood—he wasn't worth anything. He was just a no-good piece of trash nobody wanted.

Including Charlie.

Chapter Fifteen

"You good if I take off?" Scott paused outside the garage's office door.

"Yep. Thanks." Charlie's smile was brittle, but she made the attempt. "I'll see you tomorrow."

"You okay? You haven't been yourself." Understatement of the year.

"I'm okay." Or at least she was trying to be while missing Ryker and Honor like a limb had been removed from her body. Charlie would never say that to Evan, since he actually did have a below-the-knee amputation, but her emotional pain currently amounted to what she would imagine his physical pain had.

In short: it hurt.

"Thanks for checking on me. I'll see you tomorrow."

Scott took off, leaving Charlie in the quiet office, the shop scents of oil and grease and everything she usually loved doing little to comfort.

Her accountant needed numbers, so she'd figured now was as good of a time as any to make that happen. Now that she had so much extra time on her hands. Charlie had struggled to balance everything when she'd been fostering, but she would go back to that in a heart-beat if she could. She hated not knowing how Honor was doing. Hated that the girl was at the center of this weirdness between her and Ryker.

The man had eventually contacted her on Friday, but after one voice mail—which hadn't explained much of anything—and two texts, the communication had stopped, breaking her a second time around.

The short-lived attempts to reach her had left Char-lie vindicated in her beliefs that he didn't want her in their lives. If he did, he wouldn't have stopped contact-ing her. And the man definitely knew where to find her if he was determined to do so.

Obviously he was not.

Charlie's phone beeped with a text from Addie. Any-thing new?

No.

Over the last few days, they'd had the same conver-sation over and over again. Friday, Saturday and Sun-day had passed, and now it was Monday evening. Four days without Ryker and Honor had equaled forty years, and Charlie wasn't sure how she was going to make it through another lonely evening.

Her phone signaled another text. You two are the most stubborn people I've ever met! At least I told Evan my feelings. You both just refuse to recognize yours.

Charlie wasn't denying her feelings. She just didn't believe Ryker's were the same as hers. When Evan had helped Addie remodel the bed-and-breakfast last spring, she'd taken almost the whole time they'd worked to-gether to reveal a secret she'd been keeping from him for ten years. So who was she to talk? Thankfully Charlie kept that snarky bit to herself. It had made sense for Addie to be freaked out about telling Evan everything. Charlie understood that. She was just all sorts of angry and defensive right now. Even with her best friend.

A new message arrived. Pease, pease talk to the man.

Ack. Addie using Sawyer's version of the word *please* was a low blow. She knew Charlie was a softy when it came to anything involving the little guy.

But what was there to talk about? The radio silence coming from Ryker didn't need CliffsNotes to be understood.

A faint, quiet call came from the direction of the shop. Charlie popped up from the desk and made her way into the space.

"Hello? Is someone here?"

Honor stepped out from the shadows near the back entrance.

"Hey, Honor." Charlie advanced slowly in her direction, because she resembled a baby bunny about to bolt at the first sign of trouble. How had Honor gotten here? And did anyone know her whereabouts? Maybe Ryker was outside and had let her come in by herself so that he could avoid Charlie. She internally rolled her eyes.

She knelt in front of Honor. "Are you okay? What's going on?"

"You said we were going to be friends, but you lied." The quiet accusation slayed Charlie. "Where have you been?"

Stewing in my own fear and hurt. "I'm so sorry, Honor. I want to see you. So much. There's just been some…adult stuff going on. It has nothing to do with you, though, and I'm sorry that I let it affect me getting to see you." *Oh, God, what did I do? How could I have let my insecurities and uncertainties keep me from this girl?* Embarrassment at her juvenile actions swamped Charlie. So much for being fiercely capable. In this instance, she'd failed fiercely. So what if Ryker didn't want to be involved with her romantically? She'd been Team Honor from the start, and she wasn't going to let anything stop her from continuing to love the girl.

Even the personal torment of being near Ryker and knowing he didn't care for her the way she did for him.

How ironic—Charlie had been so concerned over Honor's budding friendship with Gabby turning sour and hurting her. Yet Charlie was the one who'd botched things up and accomplished that feat.

Honor's sad eyes about knocked Charlie over from her kneeling perch. "My mom is back." What? What was she talking about? "I got to see her for a little bit." Honor demolished her fingernail. "Uncle Ry says I can't live with her right now because she was sick, and she has to get all the way better first."

Oh my. That was a lot for a five-year-old to process. "You can trust your uncle, Honor. He cares about you so much. He'll take care of you and help your mom, too, I'm sure." Speaking of. "Does Uncle Ry know you're here?"

After two beats, her head slowly shook from side to side. Charlie's pulse panicked. She stood and took Honor's hand, leading her toward the office and her cell phone.

"I'm just going to let him know where you are so he doesn't worry."

Charlie quickly formed a text. Honor is at the shop. She must have walked down. She's safe and fine.

Ryker didn't answer right away, so Charlie made Honor a cup of hot chocolate and settled her on the office chair that spun and rolled, which she'd always liked. Charlie asked her about school and Gabby, and Honor told her they'd made a new friend in Ruby Wilder. Charlie rejoiced over the news, each minute with the girl melting the ache that had lodged inside her the day Honor had moved in with Ryker and she'd begun missing both of them.

Honor should never have been put in the middle of their issues, and Charlie was bound and determined not to repeat that mistake again. When she saw Ryker, she'd work out a deal with him so that she could be involved in Honor's life even if she wasn't in his.

Her phone beeped. What?! She must have taken off while I was in the shower. I thought she was in her room watching a movie.

She's fine. Charlie's fingers paused over the keys. I'll walk her back to you. We'll be there shortly.

After Honor finished her hot chocolate and Charlie promised that they wouldn't go so long without seeing each other again, they began the two-block trek. If Ryker put up a fight about her seeing Honor, Charlie wasn't sure what she would do. Maybe throw a tantrum. Or kick him in the shins. Something mature like that.

When they got to Ryker's place, he was sitting on the front step. "Honor Sloan Delaney." He scooped up the girl and held her tight. "Don't do that again. Please. You freaked me out."

"I'm sorry." Honor's reply was muffled against Ryker's sweatshirt. It was cool out but not freezing. Thankfully Honor had donned her jacket before she'd made the walk to Charlie's.

"Why did you take off like that?" Ryker set her down.

"You told me I'd see Charlie." She glanced between them. "You both did. You said nothing would change, but everything did."

Charlie's stomach churned. She met Ryker's gaze for the first time in four days and saw the same regret and pain that had to be brimming from hers.

"You're right." Ryker smoothed a hand over Honor's hair, sending her curls bouncing. "I'm sorry. We'll do better. I promise."

"Me, too." Charlie vowed to make her words true this round since she'd failed miserably on the last. When she'd signed up to foster, she'd been so green, so full of innocence. Never would she have imagined that she would disappoint a child the way she had Honor.

"Okay. Can I finish watching my movie now?" Guess they'd appeased Honor's concerns.

"Sure," Ryker answered her, but his vision stayed glued to Charlie.

"Can I have a snack while I watch?"

"Sure."

"Can I have a Popsicle?"

"Sure."

Honor skipped into the duplex, leaving Ryker and Charlie alone.

"Can I have a pony?"

At Charlie's request, Ryker's mouth eased into a grin. "Sure."

She laughed, surprised by her ability to. "Listen, Ryker, I get that you're good to go in terms of us. That you're done with a relationship with me now that you have Honor, but we really can't do this to her again. She needs me, at least while she's adjusting. We have to figure out a way for me to spend time with her. I understand that you might not want to see me, but you'll do what's best for her, right?"

Ryker's eyes had narrowed as she'd continued talking. "I never once said I didn't want you involved with Honor. In fact, I'd always planned on the opposite."

"Good. Then we can work out a schedule." *And then I can get out of here. Because being near you is even harder than I imagined it would be.*

Before this encounter, Charlie had assumed she was in *like* with Ryker. But seeing him blew that theory to bits and pieces. Somewhere along the way, she'd gone from *like* to *love*. And since that had never happened to her before, she didn't have a clue how to get out of it.

Or if escape was even possible.

Charlie was about to make a break for it, and for the sake of his beat-up heart, Ryker should probably let her. Only, something she'd said had caught him off guard, and hope had risen up with it.

"Tell me, before you go, when and how did you get the impression that I don't want a relationship with you and that I'm…*done* with you?" Wasn't that how she'd put it? And how had she ever come up with something so completely off base?

If anyone was done with someone, it was her with him. She was the one who hadn't returned his call or texts. She'd gone dark. Not the other way around.

"After Honor's care was transferred to you and I didn't hear from you until Friday, I assumed we'd been a mistake. That all you wanted was Honor and you'd gotten her out of the deal."

Huh. "My sister showed up that night. She wanted

to talk about Honor and everything that had happened while she was gone. She wanted to see Honor, but I had to tell her she couldn't stay. We had to meet up with Angela the next morning to figure things out. That's why I couldn't contact you to thank you for what you did. For the furniture. For..." He swallowed, not sure how far to go down that lane. "Kaia plans to work on regaining custody of Honor, and I said I'd help her. And then I'm going to stick around to make sure Honor's always okay. I'm not leaving Westbend. And just to set the record straight, I was never done with us. I had stuff come up with Kaia, yes, but I was never...done. You were the one who finished us."

A mouse-like squeak escaped from her. "But I thought the kiss didn't mean anything to you. That I was just a pawn, an avenue to Honor."

"The kiss meant something to me." To him it had been their beginning, but Charlie had been doubting everything behind it.

Tell her how you feel. How much you care about her. Instead his mind filled with the verbal abuse—the swearing, the yelling, the ridicule. The way Bruce would toss his beer bottle at Ryker's back or even head when he'd been walking out of a room. *Don't. Don't go there. He doesn't own me.* Ryker fought up through the sludge to find the truth, to see himself the way God saw him. "I need you, Charlie." He wanted to add more, but fear seized his vocal cords.

"You need me to help you with Honor?"

"No. I mean yes, but no. I need you for me."

"But I thought..." Charlie's teeth pressed into her lip. "I didn't know."

"How could you not? Even when I was trying not to

fall for you, my feelings were still apparent. Just ask Addie. She called me out, big-time. This thing with us isn't about Honor. At least not for me. I mean, yes, she brought us together, and yes, she's important and I want both of us to support her, but it's not all about her. I'm in love with you." The idea that she might not love him back was paralyzing. Rejection had always tormented him. But Ryker couldn't be a wuss about this. Not about Charlie. Not after all she'd done. Not with who she was. He had to rise up to her kind of strength. "And if you don't feel that way about me, I'll survive. Somehow. Because you have to be in Honor's life. We promised her as much, and we can't fail her again."

Charlie's eyes brimmed with moisture, and her face that usually gave him all the answers wasn't revealing anything. Ryker's stomach crashed to his boots.

"I want that." He had to lean forward to catch her whisper.

"Which part?"

"Both of you. But I'm afraid."

"Of what?"

"That I love you."

He laughed even as his lungs squeezed. "Why would you ever be afraid of that?"

"Because I don't know how to do this." She toggled her finger between them. "I've never been in a real relationship. I don't know how to trust that someone wants to be in one with me."

The fact that she was opening herself up quickly thawed the pieces of Ryker that had frozen during their separation.

He snagged her wrist and tugged her in his direction. "We'll figure it out together. Because I've certainly never loved anyone the way I do you." She landed against his chest willingly, and her arms wrapped around his middle. They stayed like statues for a long minute, supergluing the rift that had formed between them.

"Ryker." Charlie inched back but didn't leave his arms. Thankfully. "I'm not kidding when I say I'm naive when it comes to relationships. I didn't know what that kiss meant last week—that's part of why I was so confused. So, give it to me straight. Are we dating? Considering dating? A couple? Not there yet? I need some definition."

A smile cracked his cheeks, warming his face. Usually the relationship-defining talk came further down the road, but not with straightforward, no-nonsense Charlie. And since Ryker had no desire to run, he'd happily have it right now.

"I'm with you, Charlie. I don't care how you define it. I don't want to be with anyone else." He kissed her nose lightly, then her lips, lingering. "I don't want to kiss anyone else. I'm yours if you want me. How does that work for defining things?"

Her mouth had bowed as he'd continued talking, and now she bit her lip to stem the smile. "Good. That was pretty good."

He laughed. "So, you've had better?"

She grew serious, though her eyes sparkled with emotion and moisture and love. "Never."

Epilogue

Watching Charlotte Joy—yes, he'd learned that was her fitting middle name—Brightwood walk down the aisle made Ryker want all sorts of things. Like to call her his wife. Only this day wasn't theirs. It was Addie and Evan's…and Sawyer's, too.

Standing at the front of the church next to Addie, Charlie glowed, happiness for her friend spilling from her. She was captivating.

Charlie pointed a finger partially hidden behind her bouquet in the direction of the bride and groom, as if to admonish Ryker that he should be studying the couple getting married and not her.

He raised an eyebrow, sending her a silent message back. *You're the only one I want to look at. Deal with it.*

Her cheeks pinked, and they engaged in matching grins at the unspoken conversation passing between them. And then Honor, who was sitting next to him, climbed into his lap for a better view.

"I like weddings." Her whisper was full of awe. She'd already declared Addie's dress a princess dress and said she wanted one. No doubt Honor would have a line of men vying for her attention someday. As her uncle, Ryker planned to delay that as long as possible.

Yesterday, Kaia had finally earned her first unsupervised visit with Honor. She'd been making progress with the court system, and for the last month, she'd held a job cleaning homes and businesses again. Ryker was proud of her, and he was grateful for the way Honor blossomed with each bit of headway Kaia made. The process was slow moving, but that was a good thing. It allowed time for Kaia to prove she'd truly changed. Time for Honor to feel safe about the whole thing. To know that he wasn't going anywhere, even when her mom did regain custody.

Addie and Evan exchanged vows as Sawyer, dressed in a miniature navy-blue suit coat and tan trousers, attempted to do a somersault next to them. They laughed and then continued as if the disruption didn't matter. And it didn't to them. Not when they were becoming a family.

Ryker was strangely jealous. Though he'd only been dating Charlie for a couple of months, in his mind, they were heading *here*. He just wasn't sure how fast or slow they'd arrive.

After the food and cake, the music started, and he forced Charlie onto the dance floor. She'd claimed she couldn't dance. He'd see about that.

"I'm not liable if I step on your toes, Ry. Chances are pretty good that's going to happen."

"You sound like a business owner with the liability talk."

Her mouth curved, and her shoulders elevated in answer. "I am what I am. And when Addie and Evan got into a disagreement over whether there should be dancing at their reception, I have to say I sided with Evan. Some of us just don't have rhythm."

"Good thing you have me then. I'll take my chances."

She demolished his toes twice in the first twenty seconds, but after that, they found the right tempo. There wasn't much that they couldn't figure out together. Though Charlie was still just as out of his league as she had been at the start of all this. And yet, she loved him. Chose him. The kid who'd constantly strived to discard the messages he'd received during his childhood had been given a new story, a new message.

And Charlie's beliefs about him were eerily similar to God's. He was worthy. He was loved. He had value.

Ryker would forever thank God for the day he'd met Charlie, and the subsequent days that followed. He was half a man without her, and she made him whole in a way no one ever had before.

He nodded toward Addie's parents, who were sitting at one of the tables, amused by something Sawyer had said or done. "How's it going with them?"

Charlie had filled him in as to why Addie had struggled to get along with her mom and dad—how her parents had demanded she hide a pregnancy from Evan when the two of them had been in high school. Sounded as if the road back to harmony had been long and hard fought.

"Good so far. Addie said they've been pretty gracious and have been doting on Sawyer. I feel like if God can heal that rift, what can't He do?"

"Amen." They danced for a full song, Charlie's wrists looped around his neck, her head relaxed against him. Neither of them made a move to switch off the dance floor when the next one began, especially since Honor was happily occupied in the corner with a group of kids who were sneaking extra pieces of cake. She looked beautiful in her pink dress and shiny black shoes. She giggled about something one of the kids said, her curls bouncing, fingers covering her bowed lips.

"I asked God for a child." Charlie peered up at him. "Did I ever tell you that? For my thirtieth birthday wish/ prayer. And instead He gave me you."

"I'm…sorry?"

She laughed. "I'm not. God surprised me with His answer, but you're exactly what I needed and wanted. I just didn't know it."

"Me, too." He kissed her forehead. "I want kids, too, you know, so you just might get that bonus wish after all."

Her eyes shimmered. "I know."

In the last two months, Charlie had taken in two foster child placements that had lasted for a weekend and a week respectively. Now she was praying about her next steps, considering taking a break as the café construction progressed and the place's setup required more of her attention. But Ryker wouldn't be surprised if God brought them back to fostering again—together. Whatever the future held and wherever God directed them, Ryker only knew for certain that he wanted to face it with Charlie by his side. He wasn't sure how he'd lived so long without understanding love like this existed. If he had known it was out there somewhere, he would have searched long and hard to find it instead of just stumbling upon it like he had.

"I don't need a ring, you know."

His feet faltered. "What?"

Charlie leaned back enough for him to fall into those

evergreen depths. "If, *someday*, you want to propose or think we should get married. No pressure." Her eyes danced right along with them. "I just want you to know that I don't need a ring. As a mechanic, I won't be able to wear it because it can be dangerous. And I'm not a diamond sort of girl anyway. Bloodshed over an object doesn't appeal to me."

Ryker swallowed, his Adam's apple no doubt bobbing like a buoy in a choppy ocean. How did Charlie read his mind like that? Just last week he'd started scrolling through websites, wondering how he was ever going to afford an engagement ring or all of the expenses that came with a wedding. He was currently paying for his place, plus he'd been covering Kaia's rent for the last two months, too. Though thankfully she could handle that on her own now that she was getting paid.

"I'll just get a package of those rubber rings," Charlie continued. "The ones that can get cut off if my finger or hand gets caught somewhere it shouldn't be in an engine."

Their dancing slowed to rush-hour speeds as Ryker reeled. "You'd really marry me without a ring? What about a fancy ceremony?"

"Do I seem like the type to want a fancy ceremony? All I want is my people. My friends, my family. You." A shrug joined her curving lips. "I'm sorry if I'm pushing things ahead. We both know I'm terrible at knowing how to do this. With all of the planning for Addie's wedding, it's just been on my mind. So I thought I'd set the record straight."

She snuggled back against him as if she hadn't just tipped his world upside down. "I guess we'll have to talk about that." Ryker pressed his smile against the top of her hair, inhaling lemons and Charlie and everything good.

Despite the subject she'd brought up, Ryker still planned to ask Charlie to marry him. But with the good news she'd just revealed, he wouldn't have to wait nearly as long to make her his wife. To be her husband. To start a life together.

"Plus it would save on rent if we were married and lived together."

Ryker tossed his head back and howled with laughter.

"What? It would!"

He kissed her and it lasted longer than a public display of affection probably should, but he'd forgotten where they were for a second. He only saw Charlie. "You unromantic woman. Stop it."

She grinned. "I'm just being honest."

"And while I appreciate that, I *am* going to ask you to marry me—and not because it will save money. So just…chill for a second."

"Okay." If her twinkling eyes held any more humor, they'd suck his soul right out of his body. "But just so you know, whenever that happens, my answer's going to be yes."

* * * * *

Dear Reader,

This story starts in a tender place—Charlie's desire for a child. The woman who longs to be a mom was heavy on my heart as I wrote this. I hope I did her story justice, as it is an unanswered ache for so many.

When I started writing this book, I had no idea how many details would go into understanding the foster care process and system. Thank you to my friend Ali who talked me through numerous (and I mean numerous) questions about foster care in Colorado. She not only gave great advice but helped me to stretch things fictionally when needed. Any mistakes are all mine.

Once again, I'm so thankful for your readership. Without you, I wouldn't get to create stories, and for that I'm so grateful. I'd love to connect with you. My latest giveaway can be found at www.jill-lynn.com/news, and I'm regularly online at www.facebook.com/JillLynn Author/ and www.instagram.com/JillLynnAuthor/.

Jill Lynn

SCENE OF THE CRIME
True Blue K-9 Unit: Brooklyn • by Sharon Dunn
Someone doesn't want forensic specialist Darcy Fields to live to testify in court. And now her case is being muddied by a possible copycat killer. Can Officer Jackson Davison and his K-9 partner keep her alive long enough to uncover who wants her silenced?

COVERT COVER-UP
Mount Shasta Secrets • by Elizabeth Goddard
Private investigator Katelyn Bradley doesn't expect to find anything amiss when she checks on a neighbor after a lurker is spotted near his house—until she foils a burglary. Now she and single father Beck Goodwin are in someone's crosshairs...and discovering what the intruder was after is the only way to survive.

FUGITIVE CHASE
Rock Solid Bounty Hunters • by Jenna Night
After her cousin's abusive ex-boyfriend jumps bail and threatens Ramona Miller's life for breaking them up, she's determined to help the police catch him—if he doesn't kill her first. Bounty hunter Harry Orlansky's on the job when he saves Ramona from his mark. But can they bring the man to justice?

FORGOTTEN SECRETS
by Karen Kirst
Left with amnesia after he was attacked and the woman with him abducted, Gray Michaelson has no clue why he's in North Carolina. But working with US marine sergeant Cat Baker, who witnessed the abduction, he plans to find the truth...especially since the kidnappers have switched their focus to Cat.

EVERGLADES ESCAPE
by Kathleen Tailer
US marshal Whitney Johnson's vacation is interrupted when drug dealers take over her wildlife tour boat and she overhears information that could destroy their operation. Evading capture by diving into the water, she washes up on Theo Roberts's land. Now if they want to live, Whitney and Theo must get out of the Everglades.

TREACHEROUS MOUNTAIN INVESTIGATION
by Stephanie M. Gammon
Years ago, Elizabeth Hart took down a human trafficking ring with a single blog post—and now someone's looking for revenge. But her ex-fiancé, Officer Riggen Price, won't let anyone hurt her...or the son he never knew he had. Can they face down her past for a second chance at a future together?

SPECIAL EXCERPT FROM

🌿

LOVE INSPIRED
INSPIRATIONAL ROMANCE

*When a television reporter must go into hiding,
she finds a haven deep in Amish country.
Could she fall in love with the simple life—
and a certain Amish man?*

Read on for a sneak preview of
The Amish Newcomer *by Patrice Lewis.*

"Isaac, we have a visitor. This is Leah Porte. She's an *Englischer* friend of ours, staying with us a few months. Leah, this is Isaac Sommer."

For a moment Isaac was struck dumb by the newcomer. With her dark hair tamed back under a *kapp*, and her chocolate eyes, he barely noticed the ugly red scar bisecting her right cheek.

Leah stepped forward. "How do you do?"

"Fine, *danke*. Where do you come from?"

"California."

"Please, sit. Both of you." Edith Byler gestured toward the table.

Isaac found himself opposite Leah and gazed at her as the family gathered around the table. When all heads bowed in silence, he found himself praying he could get to know the visitor better.

At once, chatter broke out as the family reached for food.

"We hope you'll have a pleasant stay with us." Ivan Byler scooped corn onto his plate .

"I…I'm not familiar with your day-to-day life." The woman toyed with her fork. "I don't want to be seen as a freeloader."

"What is it you did before you came here?" Ivan asked.

"I was a television journalist," she replied. Isaac saw her touch her wounded cheek and glance toward him. "But after my…my car accident, I couldn't do my job anymore."

Get 4 FREE REWARDS!

We'll send you 2 FREE Books plus 2 FREE Mystery Gifts.

Love Inspired books feature uplifting stories where faith helps guide you through life's challenges and discover the promise of a new beginning.

FREE Value Over $20

YES! Please send me 2 FREE Love Inspired Romance novels and my 2 FREE mystery gifts (gifts are worth about $10 retail). After receiving them, if I don't wish to receive any more books, I can return the shipping statement marked "cancel." If I don't cancel, I will receive 6 brand-new novels every month and be billed just $5.24 each for the regular-print edition or $5.99 each for the larger-print edition in the U.S., or $5.74 each for the regular-print edition or $6.24 each for the larger-print edition in Canada. That's a savings of at least 13% off the cover price. It's quite a bargain! Shipping and handling is just 50¢ per book in the U.S. and $1.25 per book in Canada.* I understand that accepting the 2 free books and gifts places me under no obligation to buy anything. I can always return a shipment and cancel at any time. The free books and gifts are mine to keep no matter what I decide.

Choose one: ☐ **Love Inspired Romance Regular-Print** (105/305 IDN GNWC) ☐ **Love Inspired Romance Larger-Print** (122/322 IDN GNWC)

Name (please print)

Address _____ Apt. #

City _____ State/Province _____ Zip/Postal Code

Email: Please check this box ☐ if you would like to receive newsletters and promotional emails from Harlequin Enterprises ULC and its affiliates. You can unsubscribe anytime.

Mail to the **Reader Service**:
IN U.S.A.: P.O. Box 1341, Buffalo, NY 14240-8531
IN CANADA: P.O. Box 603, Fort Erie, Ontario L2A 5X3

Want to try 2 free books from another series? Call 1-800-873-8635 or visit www.ReaderService.com.

LI20R2

Journalist! What kind of God-sent coincidence was that? He smiled. "Maybe I should have you write some articles for my magazine."

"Magazine?"

Edith explained, "Isaac started a magazine for Plain people. He uses a computer to create it. The bishop gave him permission."

"An Amish man using a computer?"

"Many *Englischers* have misconceptions of how much technology the *Leit* allows," Ivan intervened. "You won't find computers in our homes, or cell phones. But while we try to live not *of* the world, we still live *in* the world, and sometimes technology is needed to keep our businesses running. So, some bishops have decided a little technology is allowed."

"What's the magazine about?" Leah asked.

"Whatever appeals to Plain people. Farming. Businesses. Land management."

"And you want *me* to write for it?" she asked. "I don't know anything about those topics."

"But that's what a journalist does, ain't so? Learn about new topics," Isaac replied. Her opposition made him more determined. "Besides, you're about to get a crash course while you stay here. Maybe you'll learn something."

"I already said I had no intention of being a freeloader."

He nodded. "*Gut.* Then prove it. You can write me an article about what you learn."

"Sure," she snapped. "How hard could it be?"

He grinned. "You'll find out soon enough."

Don't miss
The Amish Newcomer *by Patrice Lewis,*
available September 2020 wherever
Love Inspired books and ebooks are sold.

LoveInspired.com

LIEXP0820